T0149572

New BEGINNINGS *on the Yegua*

Sequel to *Rest in* PEACE *on the Yegua*

Sheryl Kleinschmidt

authorHOUSE®

AuthorHouse™
1663 Liberty Drive
Bloomington, IN 47403
www.authorhouse.com
Phone: 1-800-839-8640

First published by AuthorHouse 3/29/2012

ISBN: 978-1-4685-6660-4 (e)
ISBN: 978-1-4685-6661-1 (sc)

Library of Congress Control Number: 2012905267

Printed in the United States of America

This book is printed on acid-free paper.

Back cover photo by Virgil Curtis.

Dedication

I WOULD LIKE TO DEDICATE New BEGINNINGS on the Yegua to my granddaughters, Kiera and Kesley, who inspired some of the scenarios in this book. They have brought much joy, love, and entertainment to our family over the years. I love you, girls. Nana

Chapter One

FALL HAS COME TO MY little piece of land on the Yegua once again. The seasons here don't come suddenly, but softly meld into each other. Autumn is actually my favorite because it brings a little respite from our extremely long, hot Texas summers.

Early this summer the Yegua went dry. I'm hoping that maybe a hurricane will blow into the Gulf and send some much-needed rain this way so she'll start flowing again. She can't "talk" to me without water, and I miss her. It probably sounds strange to hear me talk this way about a creek, but the Yegua comforts my soul much like my well-worn hiking boots comfort my feet on the wooded paths around my cabin.

The fish pond just north of the creek is going dry also and I'd really hate to loose all the bass and crappie that my son-in-law, Jack, stocked in it last spring. He said he dropped the anchor down from the rowboat last week and thinks it's still about 8 feet deep in the middle. The grandchildren really enjoy fishing and swimming in that old tank. Wish Heb was here to see that—but then, again, maybe he is.

I've really enjoyed having Sandra and her family living next door. Jack has decided to become a part-time rancher in addition to his teaching position. He's repaired all the perimeter fences in order to run some cattle on my land. So, now he and I are co-owners of a small herd of Angus. It's really exciting to see the pastures being used again after years of neglect.

Kassie, my youngest granddaughter, stays with me two days a week and goes to daycare for three days in Lexington while her mom, dad and Emma go to school. On the days I keep Kassie, we have some real adventures. We plan picnics, go for walks, or work in the garden. Her favorite pastime, however, is helping me feed the cattle.

Ever since the Tonkawa Wolf Dance took place last year, we haven't had any unusual experiences out here, but living on an old Indian campground almost guaranteed some excitement from time to time.

***

It was a warm Indian Summer day not long ago when Kassie and I took Heb's old Ford Ranger into the pasture to put out some corn and hay. Grasshoppers sprang left and right as we crossed the dry field, and a dust devil challenged us to a race. The truck's worn tires spun in the sandy loam, so I gunned the engine to avoid getting stuck. The scent of flattened horse mint seeped through the cab, making my nose twitch.

I parked the truck in the shade of an old post oak tree and rolled the windows down all the way. One of the older cows named Olivia immediately stuck her head in next to Kassie hoping for a hand-out. Kassie was delighted, but pleaded for Olivia to get out. Olivia's rough, pink tongue plastered the side of Kassie's face. Sticky slobber glistened in the sunlight as it strung between Kassie's hand and hair. "Yuck, 'livia, stop it!" she squealed

Leaving Kassie to contend with Olivia, I shut off the engine and stepped out of the truck. I hurried to climb into the bed to avoid being trampled by the hungry cattle, but my arthritic hip slowed me down. Theodore, whom I had bottle-fed as a young calf, managed to shove me forward as he greedily snorted for a hand-out. Being off-balance, my foot got caught underneath the young bull's back hoof.

"Move, it, Theodore, move it!" I screeched in agony as I hopelessly tried to push him away. He continued to snort, oblivious to the excruciating pain his weight was causing my foot. The deep sand gave a little cushion, making the situation somewhat better, but I knew I was in trouble. To make matters worse, fire ants were crawling up my pants leg!

Kassie, distracted by and petting Olivia, was unaware of my situation-- not that she could do much about it. It was then I remembered the range cubes in my pocket. I took out some and threw them a couple of yards away. Gratefully, Theodore removed himself from my boot in order to get to them before the others. Relief!! As I slowly hobbled to the driver's seat, the pain doubled, and tears pushed their way to the surface. I brushed off a few more fire ants and started the engine.

Kassie's eyes grew large as she saw my face. "Nana, why're you crying?"

"Honey, Theodore accidentally stepped on my foot and it's really hurting right now. Let's just get on back to the cabin so I can get this boot off and take a look, okay?"

The quarter mile stretch of road seemed to last forever, each bump sending me into spasms of agony.I silently prayed I could get us home without passing out.

***

Pulling that boot off wasn't easy, but with Kassie's help, it finally came off, revealing some very bruised, puffy toes and a few fire ant bites. "Kassie, go get a pillow from my bed so I can prop this foot up."

With a worried look on her little face, she quickly responded.

3

"Now, honey, do you think you can get a plastic bag from the kitchen and fill it with ice?

"Why you want ice, Nana? Want some water too?"

"Just ice, Kassie, please."

Thirty minutes later the pain had not subsided, but had only gotten worse. I was pretty sure a couple of toes were broken. Well, there wasn't much I could do at this point but stay still and wait for Sandra and Jack to come home. I turned on the cartoons for Kassie and rested.

***

Familiar voices overshadowed the continuous drone from the television and I opened my eyes to see Sandra standing over me with a concerned look on her face. "Mom, what on earth happened to you? I knocked on the kitchen door several times before Kassie finally heard me and opened it up!"

"Sandra," I painfully whispered, "am I glad to see you! I don't know, I think a couple of toes are broken. Kassie helped me out with a pillow and some ice, but it hurts like heck right now. I think you're going to have to find some Tylenol or maybe something stronger for the pain."

"I'll go home in a minute and see what I've got, but why don't you explain what you did to yourself? Maybe we shouldn't be leaving you two alone out here while we're at work!"

"Don't be ridiculous, Sandra, it's not life-threatening-- just a couple of broken toes. Ole Theodore decided he didn't want to wait long enough for me to get the corn out of the back of the truck and started pushing his weight around. Unfortunately for me, my foot was under him at the time. He's just a big, old spoiled bottle baby, that's all—didn't mean to hurt me."

"Well, the damage is done all the same, Mom, you don't need to be out here feeding the cattle by yourself.Jack can do that when he gets home from work. Right now I'll go get you some pain meds, but as soon as I feed you and the kids, we're heading to the ER."

"No, we're not!" I stubbornly resisted. "There's nothing can be done for these toes at the ER that ice, rest and Tylenol can't fix right here at home, and that's final."

Before the rebuttal came, my cell phone rang, giving me the escape I needed for the moment. "Hi, Burton," I winced into the phone as Sandra scowled.

"Burton!" Sandra blurted out as she grabbed the phone from my hand. "Please talk some sense into my mother. She's sitting here with at least two broken toes and refuses to go to the emergency room!"

I couldn't hear his response to that but Sandra continued, "..... something about one of the bulls stepping on her foot this afternoon when she went out to feed."

Another pause and then, "Thanks, Burton; see you in a little while." And with a smirk on her face, my daughter claimed some unknown victory and left the room.

***

Sandra decided to cook supper at my house so she could keep an eye on me. I was grateful, but was still convinced I did not need to see a doctor. Burton's coming over was not going to change my mind on that account.

An hour later, the savory smell of spaghetti filled the cabin, whetting my appetite. Jack and Emma had joined us by now, so Kassie and I retold the Theodore story at least twice (once from my perspective and once from hers). My foot still throbbed, but the pain meds were taking the edge off.

The kids all brought their plates to the den so I wouldn't have to move or eat by myself. Silence overcame my granddaughters' exuberant chatter as they slurped up their food. After a few bites, my son-in-law moved closer to my side and began suggesting that maybe I should avoid feeding the cattle and stay closer to the cabin while they were all at school.

"Jack, that's not even in the cards........" I started in defense of myself, but before I could continue, we all were interrupted by the slam of a truck door in the front driveway. Burton had arrived and I braced myself for yet another round of platitudes and over-protection.

Without so much as a knock on the door, Burton whisked into the room and surveyed the situation. His eyes landed on my extended foot as he drawled, "Well, what've you gotten yourself into now, Sunshine?"

"Well, hello to you, too!" I icily replied as Sandra sent an approving glance Burton's way. The two of them ganging up on me was getting to be a habit—one that I knew was out of love and concern, but nonetheless, annoyed the fire out of me!

"Ouch!" I screeched as Burton's hand probed my puffy toes. "What on earth do you think you're doing? You're an archaeologist, NOT a doctor!"

Ignoring my pain, he simply stated, "Your toes are broken."

"I know that, Einstein, so please unhand me."

"Sandra, go get me a bowl of warm water, please," Burton quietly ordered.

"What?" I began as he pulled a homespun bag from his back pocket. Without answering, he poured the contents into the water and began mixing it up with his bare hands. The smell was horrific and made my eyes water profusely.

Before I could protest, my foot was in his huge, tender hands being smeared with that gosh-awful concoction. Emma and Kassie started giggling as they held their noses and ran from the room. I didn't blame them, I wanted to run away too.

"What the heck is this nasty stuff anyway?" asked Jack as he examined the packet.

"Oh, just some ju-ju I got from Minnie when I sprained my knee a couple of years ago. Was on the phone with her discussing some Indian affair when out of the clear she said, 'Mosley, Indian medicine will heal leg. You don't see white man doctor again.'

Of course, I had not discussed my injury with her—she just somehow knew. That little old shaman showed up in my office that very day with this here bag of who knows what. Right there in front of my secretary, she got down on her knees, rolled up my pants leg and slathered this gunk all over my hairy leg. It didn't make her any difference that a smirking crowd was gathering in the hallway. She just rubbed this gunk on and wiped her hands on the front of her dress. Told me to mix it with warm water and rub it on twice a day. Without another word, she hobbled out, to the amazement of us all.

Thinking she was just a crazy old Indian, I rolled down my pant leg, shooed everyone out, and ignored their amused laughter. Much to my surprise, though, by bedtime the swelling in my knee was gone, and I was able to walk unaided by crutches in two days."

Well, after last year's experience with Minnie Williams and the Wolf Dance Ceremony, I've learned not to second-guess anything she says or does. If Burton's leg was miraculously healed, maybe my foot would be also.

Burton and I have not shared much of our other-world experiences here on the Yegua with my family. There are some things we think are best kept to ourselves.

The pain must've dulled my senses, though, because I blurted out,

"Well, if half that stuff I saw growing at Minnie's house is medicinal or magic, I ought to be running races by Wednesday!"

"Mother—you KNOW this person, this Minnie person also?" Sandra inquired suspiciously.

"Well……..yes, I went by there once with Burton when we first started dating," I covered up.

Realizing we were treading on dangerous territory, Burton calmly added, "I often converse with Minnie when I have questions in regard to her tribe, the Tonkawa. She's a fountain of information and has helped correct a lot of misinformation garnered over the years."

Placated by this added information, Sandra began cleaning up the supper dishes and moved on to the kitchen. Burton and I exchanged a knowing look and gingerly repressed a burst of laughter.

***

Sure enough, by the next morning, the swelling in my foot and toes had been reduced to almost nothing. In spite of the half-fear/half-respect I had for Minnie, I wanted to hug her neck when I realized I could walk with relatively little pain.

I had convinced everyone to go to their respective homes the night before with the promise that I would call if I needed help in any way. So, with no one there to interfere, I took myself to the kitchen and made a hearty breakfast.

As I sipped a second cup of coffee at the kitchen table, my eyes drifted out back and once again to Heb's gravesite. The crepe myrtles were in full bloom, making a beautiful backdrop to the purple fall asters circling the flowerbed. A single ray of sunshine beamed down from above, highlighting the garden bench I'd placed there the year before.

Caught up in the moment, I spoke out loud to Heb as if he were sitting across the table from me. "Heb, I am going to need to give Burton an answer soon. He's been very patient with me, but I can't keep him waiting forever. He wants us to marry before the Christmas holidays. That would give us almost a month for a honeymoon before he would have to return to his work at the University in Austin.

Bobby and Sandra love Burton and the grandchildren adore him. I've met his sons and they're wonderful young men.But, I can't help but feel like I'm betraying you in all this. Please let me know it's okay, Heb. Somehow, just tell me it'll be okay........."

My thoughts were interrupted by the kitchen phone and I grabbed it before the shrill ring pierced the silence again. "Hello," I heard my sluggish voice say.

"Good morning, Joan, how's that foot this morning?" Burton inquired.

"Mornin', Burton; it is amazingly much improved. Whatever potion Minnie mixed up should be patented and sold—it's a miracle drug for sure! I've got enough left for a couple more treatments, so think I'll be back to normal pretty soon."

"Great—toldja it would work. Listen, we need to talk. Would it be alright if I drove out there tonight and fixed supper for you? You need to stay off that foot another day or so anyway-- so whattaya say? I can grill some steaks."

Postponing "the" talk wasn't going to make things any better, so I hesitatingly agreed to Burton's supper plans. Truth be told, Burton was an excellent cook and an even better dining companion. Why I hadn't jumped at the chance to marry him was puzzling to me as well as to my children. Heb's death was no longer the painful throb it used to be, so why couldn't I make a commitment?

***

Nervously, I preened for my date with Burton. He'd been to my

9

house many times before, but tonight was important. It wasn't fair for me to put off my decision any longer.

Burton arrived just as maroon and pink sunrays fell behind the Yegua. As I opened the door, the locusts' incessant drone mixed with the tree frogs' serenade as they vied for attention. The cooling air saturated the room, signaling the end of another warm fall afternoon and the beginning of what I hoped would be a pleasant evening.

Burton's kiss was welcoming, but I could tell he meant business tonight. No teasing, no playful pinches, no exaggerated compliments....... he immediately went about the business of lighting the grill and preparing food.

I was hustled into the chaise lounge on the patio, and a fluted glass of wine suddenly appeared in my hand. With nothing to do but watch and wait, I began to relax and take in the moment. More night sounds began to creep into the scene as the smoky charcoal came alive. Welcome rain clouds began to puff themselves up like mushrooms on the horizon, and lightening illuminated them from the inside out. They reminded me of a giant jellyfish I once saw at the beach. Hopefully, they would do more than tease us with the promise of rain this evening.

Soon the grill was ready and grease was popping up from our steaks. Burton was uncharacteristically quiet tonight, engrossed in what he was doing. I used that quiet time to ask myself what I would tell him. Was I ready for another marriage? Could I let go of the past or was that even necessary? Did I want to live in Austin again, or would Burton move out here? So many unanswered questions.........

As the steaks continued to simmer, a soft misty rain began to fall around us. It began to drip off the patio cover in small droplets, making tiny volcanoes in the earth below. The sweet scent of clean air swirled around us as the rain began to ping the metal roof of the patio cover. Unruffled by the sudden weather changes, Burton pulled up another chair and brought over a small table. Before long, we were dining by candlelight and the soft rain had become a blessed downpour. We ate in silence, watched the distant lightning, and heard the Yegua sigh as she slowly came back to life.

Chapter Two

IT RAINED ALL NIGHT—A LONG, slow drenching sort of rain. I should've waken up refreshed, relieved to find my Yegua trickling (not flowing yet), and the pasture regenerated from life-giving moisture, but I didn't. I was melancholy, and with good reason.

Burton had left the night before without an answer to his proposal. He wasn't angry, just dejected and hurt. Nothing I could say or do at that point was going to improve the situation. He simply walked away with these parting words, "If or when you can make up your mind, call me. Until then, it's best I not talk to you. Goodbye, Joan."

I was numb, felt a tremendous loss and had a chill in my soul. My best friend, my companion, my champion, had walked away, and it was my own fault. But, for the life of me, I simply did not know what to do about it. Maybe some time apart would help me see things more clearly.

After breakfast I tried to plan out my day, but my thoughts were jumbled. All I could think about was Burton's sad face and my own uncertainties. At times like this I often sat out in my prayer garden visiting with Heb, but today I needed someone who could talk back. Maybe Bobby would have lunch with me. After loosing Heb, my son has become my greatest anchor in times of turmoil. Bobby seemed to be blessed with common sense and was a wonderful sounding board. Maybe what I needed was a man's point of view on the situation.

Bobby didn't answer his cell phone, so I tried his secretary at Johnston Motors in Austin. "Hi, Amber. This is Joan, how're you today?"

After a few pleasant exchanges, I continued, "Is Bobby in his office this morning? I couldn't reach him on his cell."

"Yes, Ms. Johnston, he is here but in a meeting. Could I have him call you in a little while?"

"That would be great, Amber. You might mention that I'd like to have lunch with him today so that he won't make other plans."

Being fairly certain my son would not turn down my invitation, I went ahead and got dressed to drive into Austin. Soon the phone rang, and we finalized our dining arrangements. For the first time in days, I felt a twinge of optimism.

Bobby and I met at a cafeteria not too far from his office near downtown. He saw me struggling with my sore foot and rushed to my assistance. "Hey, Mom, let me give you a hand there! Heard about you and Theodore doing a waltz together. Looks like he did a number on you."

"Yes, that spoiled, overgrown baby got me good, but it's healing up nicely. I'll just be more careful next time. He won't catch me off-guard any more, that's for sure."

Arm in arm, we walked the short distance to the cafeteria entrance. There was a slight chill in the air left from last night's rainstorm, but it comfortably matched my dour mood. I tried to be upbeat and chatty, inquired about Karen and the children, but that only lasted 'til we got our trays and sat down.

The food was enticing and smelled wonderful, but it was hard to fill my stomach when my heart was so empty.

"Mom..... Mom?"

"Yes, Son?"

"You're not eating, and that's not like you. What's up?"

"You're just like your father. I never could fool him either." I played with my napkin, twisting it into a coil before I continued, "Bobby, Burton has asked me to marry him."

"That's wonderful, Mom, and not unexpected..... so why so glum?"

"I don't know. I'm just not able to give him an answer. I love him, that's not the problem. He's agreed to live with me out at the cabin as well, so again, no problem. There's just some nagging little thing in the back of my mind that simply renders me incapable of making a decision."

"Could it be that you feel like you're cheating on Dad? You know, he'd want you to be happy. No one expects you to be alone the rest of your life. You're not too old to remarry."

"I don't think so, Bobby. Heb and I always had an understanding that if something happened to one of us, we wouldn't want the remaining spouse to be alone. Every now and then there's a smidgen of guilt, but nothing that would keep me from marrying Burton."

"You know that Sandra and I love Burton, and our families have become very fond of him as well. Please don't think for a minute that we wouldn't all be happy for both of you."

"I know, Bobby, thank you. I just wish I could put my finger on the problem and erase all doubt from my mind. Whatever it is, I know it has nothing to do with Burton himself, although I'm sure he is wondering. He doesn't even want to see me or talk to me until I know what I want to do-- and that makes me miserable. The last thing I want to do is hurt him."

"Well, Mom, if you want my opinion, I think you should marry Burton. He adores you and will make a fine husband. I'm sure whatever is bothering you will take care of its self in the long run. Surely it's not important enough to keep you from being with the second love of your life."

And, with a twinkle in his eye, he added, "Besides, maybe it isn't too late for me to get that little brother I always wanted!"

"Young man, you just mind your own business!" I threw back at him, but secretly laughed at the absurdity of that idea.

A half hour later, Bobby escorted me back to my car, and I drove away feeling much better about my dilemma. I knew in my heart of hearts that marrying Burton would be the best thing that could happen to me and determined to let him know very soon. Yes, I would call him tonight and ask him to come over the next evening for supper. This time I would cook for him AND give him my answer.

***

Sitting in my recliner back at the cabin, I iced down my foot and then reapplied the last of Minnie's potion to my sore toes. The evening news was on and had my rapt attention until I heard a knock on my back door. "Come in!" I yelled.

My son-in-law, Jack, lumbered through the kitchen and into the den. "Hey, Joan, how's that foot a doin?"

"Better than expected, Jack. I saw you out feedin' the cattle a little earlier. Everything okay? Didja give ole Theodore a piece of my mind while you were out there?"

"The cattle're fine, and looks like the rain is greenin' up the pasture, so we may get to cut back on the hay soon. Theodore's his usual pesky self, so I've been puttin' hay out in several locations to give everyone else a chance ta eat."

"The weather forecast's predicting more rain, so maybe the tank and the Yegua'll both fill up soon. I was beginning to think we'd have to start running water out to the cattle before long," I added.

"Joan, I walked 'round the tank dam on my way back to the house a little while ago. There's wolf tracks all over the north side. I'm a little concerned so I'll keep an eye peeled. The last thing we need's a wolf out there chasin' our cattle or killin' calves. Emma and Kassie are still small enough to be attacked as well. With the drought, he's probably just thirsty, but who knows?"

My ears heard Jack's words, but my heart leaped into my throat. No way-- would Lobo be back for some unknown reason? Is this what my woman's intuition had been telling me? Maybe my fear had nothing at all to do with marrying Burton, but with another visit from that "other" world.

Before I could reply, Jack buzzed my cheek with a stubbly kiss and headed out the door. As the screen slammed, I heard Kassie and Emma squealing in delight and wondered what those two girls had found this time. It seemed they never tired of nature's offerings whether it be caterpillars, doodlebugs or butterflies. More than once I've had to come to their rescue, or the rescue of a hapless critter clutched in little fingers.

The answer came in the form of a "Woof, woof," and I thought to myself, "Uh oh, that sounds like trouble."

Removing my foot from the pillow, I hobbled over to the window in time to see the girls hugging the scraggliest dog I think I'd ever seen. Jack was desperately trying to pry them off the overjoyed pooch in order to check him over. Kassie and Emma were forced to go sit on their front porch while the inspection was made. Sandra came out the door carrying a bowl of water which she placed in front of the dehydrated animal.

Apparently the decision to take in this poor creature was made, because he was soon fed, watered, and back in the girls' arms. Glad to know he was their problem and not mine, I hobbled back to the recliner and watched "Wheel of Fortune". On many days I out-guessed the contestants, but tonight my mind was elsewhere........

***

Early the next morning, I limped to the backyard to put corn out by the creek. It was quiet except for the chatter of a couple of squirrels playing tag around an old mossy oak whose roots stuck out of the bank on the opposite side of the Yegua. It was good to see things start to come back to life after the long, harsh summer. My shoes were covered in the morning's dew, causing sand to attach itself like iron filings on a magnet.

On my walk back to the house, I decided to sit in the prayer garden and watch the sun rise in the east while my shoes dried. If I was lucky, maybe I'd see a deer or two come out for the corn. The resident mockingbird started up her morning cantor as honking geese were heard high over my head. Yes, Fall was making her debut—none too soon in my book.

While sitting and contemplating the joys of the morning, I remembered the call made to Burton last night. He didn't answer, but I know he heard the message I left asking him to come out for supper tonight. I intended to pledge my undying love for him and surrender my heart in the promise of marriage. He wouldn't return my call, but he would come.

Suddenly, my reverie was rudely interrupted by the shrill bark of a dog. Quickly looking up, I saw that same, sad dog from yesterday crawl out from under Jack and Sandra's back porch. He was looking toward the creek and barking as if there were no tomorrow, but when my eyes searched the woods' brushy edge, I saw nothing.

"Cooter, hush up!" came Jack's deep voice from their back door. Cooter—now that was a funny name indeed. Wonder which one of the girls came up with that one?

Jack came out the door and walked down to the creek in the direction that Cooter was staring. The mutt timidly walked behind him, all the while his hair standing at attention along his skinny backbone.

On his way back to the house, Jack spied me sitting in the garden and came over as Cooter went back to his porch retreat. "Mornin', Joan. Looks like our wolf's back. There's fresh prints all over the creek bed. Didn't see anything did you?"

"Nope, all I've seen this morning are two squirrels, a mockingbird—and that mangy dog you're calling Cooter! Are you planning on keeping him?"

"What choice do I have? Sandra and the girls've already bathed 'em, named 'em and made 'em a bonifide member of the family! Besides, with that wolf out there, it won't hurt to have an extra pair of eyes and ears 'round here!"

"Well, he does seem to be protecting his territory already. Guess I'll have to mosey over and make friends with him soon so he won't be trying to chase me off!"

***

Later that evening, Cooter could be heard baying at Burton's truck as it came up the driveway. I figured Burton could handle Cooter alright and hurried to put the finishing touches on the candle-lit table in front of the fireplace. The wine was cooling, and empty plates sat in anticipation of being filled.

Before opening the door, I turned off the lights, allowing the candles to provide the appropriate ambiance in the cozy room. Clear "fairy" lights twinkled on the mantle, hinting of the holiday season not too-far distant.

Burton knocked a second time before I could get to the door, but I wasn't in a hurry tonight. Tonight was a night of decision, not indecision—no second guessing, no doubts. Romance was in the air.........

As I opened the door, Burton's face lit up. He knew. He just knew, and a huge smile spread across his handsome face for the first time in weeks. Like a schoolgirl, I jumped into his open arms and planted a big, old wet kiss on his firm lips.

Hungrily, he returned my kiss and squeezed me until I thought I would burst. I was afraid to move, but soon Burton's arms began to tremble and he had to put me down. "Joan, how/when/why?" he stuttered as gentle tears trickled down his manly face.

Now I was tearing up as well, but all that mattered was that we were going to be married and I, for one, wasn't going to let anything get in the way. "Burton, I've known that I loved you for a long time, but there was some nagging premonition in the back of my mind that wouldn't give me peace about marrying you until now."

"So what's changed?"

"I think Lobo's back!"

"You're kidding!"

"No. Jack's been finding tracks for a couple of days now. He thinks it's a lone wolf finding respite from the drought, but I know in my heart it's Lobo. I can FEEL his presence even though I haven't actually seen him. Something is wrong, Burton, but the good thing is that I know it has nothing to do with my marrying you."

A few moments passed before we sat down at the table with our plates loaded and our hearts even fuller. A toast was shared and before I knew it, my future husband was down on one knee beside me.His lips brushed my hand as he picked it up and held it tight. "Joan, Johnston, will you make me the happiest man in the world and be my wife?"

"Of course," was all I could get out. Heartfelt promises were sealed with a kiss as the familiar lightheartedness we had always shared returned full-fold. My face glowed with an internal joy known only to someone lucky enough to find love—twice.

Mid-way through our engagement meal we were interrupted by sudden, violent howls surging up from the Yegua. "That's him!" I yelled as Burton ran out the back door. He and Jack met out back and raced toward the creek in an attempt to spy the lone creature. Cooter was barking fiercely, but all the while backing away from the real danger. Maybe some day he'd get some courage, but for now he felt he'd done his part. I didn't blame him.

When Burton returned, he had a worried look on his face. "Joan, I think you're right about Lobo. From the vicinity of the howls, he was right here on your side of the creek, but neither Jack nor I could see a thing. It seems the dog was able to see him though.

I may try to get in touch with Minnie tomorrow. If this is Lobo, his reappearance could be quite significant. This ground is still sacred to the Tonkawa so he may always be drawn to this area. Maybe Minnie will have some insight as to what is taking place this time. I'm just glad that Jack and Sandra live next door so you won't be facing this out here alone. And, if you'll agree to be my wife before Christmas, I'll soon be by your side as well!"

Chapter Three

I WAS UP EARLY THE next morning, coffee in hand and headed for my prayer garden. As I looked up, I noticed that Sandra and Jack were up early this bright Saturday morning and decided to go over with my good news.

As I approached, I saw that Cooter now had a pallet and was sleeping on top of the porch instead of under it. He and I looked each other over and made a truce while I knocked on the back door. "You are one sad-looking pooch," I muttered under my breath, "but, you are one lucky pooch, for sure. This little family will love you unconditionally and spoil you rotten."

Sandra opened the door and groggily motioned me inside. "Mornin', Mom. Making social calls early today, aren't you?" she teased.

Ignoring her jibe, I plopped myself down on a barstool and pushed aside an assortment of books, magazines and toys to make room for my coffee. Jack strolled through the kitchen about that time, so I asked him to join us. I assumed the girls were still sleeping since the TV was silent-- as well as the rest of the house.

"I have an announcement to make," I mumbled through a slurp

of coffee. Sandra started giggling while Jack unsuccessfully tried to shush her.

Before I could get in another word, she blurted out, "You accepted Burton's proposal last night, didn't you?"

"Now how on earth would you know that?" I countered.

"Because she was spying on y'all with binoculars!" Jack interjected amidst a barrage of punches to his mid-section.

Jack jumped aside to avoid more punches and kicked over a sack of dog food leaning against the refrigerator. "Okay, okay—truce!" he begged as he began to sweep up the mess.

"Sandra, you didn't!" I accused with pretended insult.

"Well, if you don't want me watching, close the curtains next time! So, when's the big date?"

"We haven't decided for sure, but it will be early to mid- December so Burton will have off for our honeymoon. The wedding won't take much planning since it'll be here in the back yard in the gazebo. Burton'll take care of the honeymoon plans and I'll be the wedding planner."

"You don't mind a little help, do you? Decorating should be a piece of cake because of the holidays. And, speaking of cake—doesn't Marge Kaufman bake wedding cakes? Seems I overheard her talking about that at church the other day. Bobby and Jack can barbeque and we can order the sides….."

I just let her go on and on, not really listening, but taking in the joy she got out of planning MY wedding!

***

A couple of nights later, we had all decided to have a weiner roast down by the creek. It was a harvest moon night, the Yegua was half-full and flowing, and Burton had come down for the evening. We had invited my neighbors, Marge and Alfons, over to join us, so we had quite a ring of chairs around the fire pit.

Every now and then another cicada cranked up its little chainsaw and joined the buzzing of its friends. Smoke spiraled up into the sky as our skewed sausages sputtered and began to split open.We all passed around a new bottle of wine Burton had picked up on his way to help celebrate our engagement with friends and family.

Kassie and Emma intermittently chased frogs and played fetch with Cooter, who was beginning to show signs of a pot belly in spite of his still-ragged appearance.

"Ya, da cattle prices should oughta be goin down now dat we got some goot rain, Jack. But, on da udder han, ve von't hafta be feedin so much —at least til it freezes," assured Alfons.

Marge and Sandra were engrossed in wedding cake talk, so Burton and I were left to ourselves. Hands entwined, we just sat and enjoyed the comfortable camaraderie of family and friends when suddenly everything came to an abrupt halt.

I don't know whether it was the full moon or the lure of the smoking wieners that drew in this creature, but the loudest, eeriest howl I'd ever heard came deep from the woods on the other side of the creek. Jack was on his feet in an instant yelling for Kassie and Emma to get back to the fireside as Cooter darted into the thick brush.

"Cooter, Cooter!" the girls screamed in chorus, but the surprisingly brave little dog disappeared into the darkness. Jack and Burton grabbed the girls and drug them to the safety of our campfire while Alfons hobbled to his truck and grabbed a rifle. The men quickly found flashlights and headed into the woods after Cooter.

All of us women huddled around the fire, holding onto Emma and Kassie for dear life. We should've headed for the cabin, but we were still in shock and too scared to move. We could hear Cooter barking for all he was worth deep inside the dense covering. Eyes locked and ears cocked, we continued to wait for what seemed an eternity. Finally, Alfon's rifle sounded out in an echoing boom-boom-boom!

After that, there was silence. Minutes turned into a quarter hour, and then a half before footsteps and voices could be heard returning to our side of the Yegua. We had already gathered more wood and put it on the fire to help guide our men back to us. A few mosquitoes were making their presence known, but we were too frightened to pay them much mind.

Eventually, we saw Burton and Alfons making their way into the knee-deep water. Then, they turned and helped Jack who was carrying Cooter. Jack's shirt was drenched in blood. Cooter's head hung limply on Jack's shoulder.

Sandra saw what was going on and tried to hurry the girls into the house before they got a glimpse of their beloved pet, but it was too late. "Mommy, Mommy, we don't wanna go inside, we wanna see Cooter!" screamed Emma. By now Kassie was upset as well and crying her little eyes out.

"Cooter's bleedin', Mommy. He's gonna die!" wailed Kassie with huge eyes.

As soon as the men reached our side of the creek, I called out, "Bring him over to my patio. I'll get my first aid kit and we'll have a look at at 'em!"

With haste, we set up a make-shift ER on my picnic table. Jack held Cooter as I gently washed away blood, hair and dirt. The miserable little dog whined with each touch, but was good as gold. Some animals bite out of fear, but this little guy had already had such a rough life that he was appreciative of even the least attention, even if it hurt.

Alfons came over to assess the situation. "Joan, let me hava lookit 'em. Not much ah hadn't seen out'n these woods over da years."

Those giant hands began to gently probe the little dog's mangled hind leg as Cooter's rough tongue routinely licked up the oozing blood. Alfons stroked Cooter's head and quietly whispered words of encouragement to him. The sight brought tears to my eyes.

I searched the faces of the little group huddled around the table. Marge stood back a bit and chewed her bottom lip. Burton's eyes were focused on Alfon's hands, and Jack wore a frown of deep concern. I don't think any one of us had taken a breath until the examination was complete.

Finally Alfons made an announcement, "E's gonna be okay I tink. Ve yust gotta set dat leg. He ain't gonna like it none, so Joan, get us sometin to make a muzzle vith. Ve'll doctor da puncture wounds at da same time."

Forty-five minutes later, Cooter's leg was set, splinted and cleaned up. It was decided that he would stay with me over-night so that Emma and Kassie wouldn't disturb him or be upset if he cried out in pain.

The men were pretty certain that the animal Cooter encountered in the woods was a panther. There weren't any footprints because of the deep leaf mold on the forest floor, but it seemed that Cooter had been knocked down and attacked from above. Alfons also said that the animal's scream was typical of a panther, not a wolf. The guys must've scared him off in the nick of time or Cooter would've been a goner.

After Cooter was fed and situated on an old blanket on my den floor, everyone went home except Burton. As he held me tightly in his arms he said, "Joan, after tonight I'll be even more relieved when we're married and I'm living out here. I know Jack's a good man and very protective, but there's strength in numbers and it'll take all of us working together to stay safe. So, what do you say we move the wedding up a couple of weeks?"

A soft smile came over my face as I realized how much this man cared for me. He not only cared for me, but for my family and friends as well. I silently thanked God for sending him into our lives. As I nestled my head deep into his shoulder, I replied, "I think that would be a good idea, Burton."

***

Very early the next morning, I awoke to Cooter's pitiful whining. He was desperately trying to hobble to the door. The poor creature must be aching to relieve himself. I gingerly helped him out and stayed nearby to assist if he needed help.

After a few steps, Cooter discovered he could maneuver better on three legs and held the injured leg at an angle. Then, without warning and not even a lingering look, Cooter scooted off to his own back porch and took himself right up the steps! Now that was one tough puppy! I made a mental note to start saving him some choice scraps from my own table from now on. In my opinion, Cooter had earned himself some guardian angel wings the night before when he put himself between my grandbabies and that panther. Who knows what might've happened if he hadn't been there?

Later that day I received a phone call from Burton saying he'd contacted a game warden in Lee County. He'd heard some other reports about a possible mountain lion or panther in my area. There hadn't been any visual confirmations as of yet—just the nighttime screams and animal remains such as feathers, rabbit pelts, etc. The good news was that the huge cats didn't stay long in one place, and their hunting grounds were quite extensive. So, with any luck, our cat moved on out of the area after being chased and shot at.

Just the same, I determined to keep a close watch on my surroundings, my cattle and my grandchildren!

***

The following Monday, I decided my foot was well enough to start feeding again and took the Ranger out to the field loaded with corn and range cubes. Jack had put out some round bales earlier, but I still liked to have a little "hands-on" with the cattle to keep them tame and used to me.

I kept one eye on Theodore and stayed one step ahead of him this time. As I threw corn out of the back of the truck, I noticed footprints in the damp sand that were definitely not made by the cattle. For the life of me, they looked like Lobo's except that they were smaller. They couldn't belong to Cooter, either, because he was still hopping around on three legs and a splint.

I would be sure to mention this to Jack when he got home, but there wasn't much I could do about it now. Looks like that wolf had stuck around after all.

Out of curiosity, and because there wasn't anything else I needed to do, I decided to take a drive up around the north end of my property. My foot was healed enough to walk, but with a panther and a wolf on the loose, I felt safer in my truck. The acreage north of the tank was more or less hidden behind the tank dam and a small, tree-lined ravine which had to be crossed on a make-shift bridge. Heb had meant to rebuild that old bridge, but passed away before he had the chance.

As I approached the bridge, I slowed down, making sure the truck tires lined up with the boards. It was a bit tricky, but I felt it could be done well enough. Besides, the ravine wasn't that deep. What would be the worst thing that could happen? Most of the water had already flowed into the Yegua, so I wasn't worried about drowning.

Slowly, inch-by-inch, I crept across the wooden span. My knuckles had a death grip on the steering wheel, but other than that, I was okay. Finally, my tires reached solid ground on the opposite side and I breathed a sigh of relief. Speeding up now, I began to look over my property. It was a beautiful piece of bottom land alright. I spied some mustang grapevines on the fence that still held a few clusters of fruit in their grasp. Maybe it wasn't too late to make some jelly after all…….. and there, on my left, stood that big, old native pecan tree in the northwest corner. If the crows and squirrels left any nuts behind, I might bake some pies for the upcoming holidays.

Soon I reached the north fence, turned around, and headed for home.It was downhill all the way to the ravine. I got distracted by a cottontail I'd scared up out of a patch of tall grass, and picked up speed. Fortunately for me, something else caught my attention and slowed me down. Calmly sitting in the middle of the bridge was a wolf--a white wolf. At first I thought it was Lobo, but this looked like a female—much smaller. There we sat, staring at each other. Something was familiar about her, but I couldn't put my finger on it. Grey hair mixed in with the white, letting me know she was definitely not a pup.

Slowly, she turned to walk away, and as she did, she disappeared into thin air. "No, no, no!" I screamed as I realized she was only a spirit just as Lobo had been. Why won't you leave me alone? Haven't I done enough for you already?"

In agony, I opened the truck door and climbed out. I beat the hood of the truck with my fists and screamed angrily. This was not what I wanted to see or deal with again, for that matter.

Still in disbelief, I gingerly walked to the spot where the wolf had sat on the bridge. My shoe hit a soft spot and I almost went through the rotten plank. Had I continued in the Ranger, I certainly would've gone through and fallen into the gulley. It's amazing I made it across the first time. She had protected me, but why? And how was I going to get the Ranger home?

After further thought, I decided to drive down the ravine a ways to look for another place to cross. It was either that, or walk home. It wasn't that far, but I didn't feel comfortable leaving the truck out in the pasture overnight. Besides, the coons would wreak havoc with the rest of the corn in the truck bed if it were left for long.

After a couple of trips up and down the gulley, I decided on a spot to cross. Putting the truck in low gear, I crept down and out the other side with little trouble. It was a good thing we'd had some rain recently or I would've gotten stuck in the sandy bottom.

***

After supper, I called Burton at his house in Austin. "Hey, there," I started, "you won't believe what happened to me today." I gave him a blow-by-blow account of the afternoon, ending with sighting the new phantom wolf.

"You're kidding, right?" he exclaimed.

"I wish I were, Burton, but she disappeared into thin air. I'm assuming she, at least I think it's a she, like Lobo, comes from the mysterious world of the Tonkawa, but what on earth could she want with me? Surely there aren't any more murdered Indians buried on my property!"

"Well, I guess it's time to contact Minnie Williams again. If anyone can solve this puzzle, it will be her."

Chapter Four

I HAD AGREED TO DRIVE into Austin to meet Burton at the mall to do a little shopping for our honeymoon cruise and then out to eat. Neither of us had been on a cruise before, so we were excited. The Caribbean was our destination, and we were determined not to let our age hinder us from participating in all offered experiences—including snorkeling. So, we shopped for new swimsuits, sunglasses, sandals—the works. Oh my, we were going to be geeky!

During our meal, Burton related how he'd tried to get in touch with Minnie during the day, but was unsuccessful. No sooner than he'd told me this, his phone rang.

"Burton Mosley here," his deep baritone voice answered. Apparently he thought it was a business call since no name registered when he answered. As he listened to the caller, his face took on a very serious demeanor as he struggled to hear above the din of the restaurant. "Just a minute, let me go outside where I can hear you better."

While Burton was gone, I searched my mind to figure out who the mystery caller was. Worry took over, and I was concerned that something had happened to one of Burton's sons. Michael was still in the Air Force, and he was the one I was most concerned about. Sean was living in the states, but his job kept him traveling a lot as well. I played with my salad and took a few bites of my steak, but my appetite was gone.

Finally, Burton returned to our table obviously disturbed. I took his hand and asked, "Who was it? Are Michael and Sean okay?"

"No, no, the boys are fine. That was John Williams. He said that Minnie has been missing for about a week. The police have been called in and they're starting to suspect foul play. The police are monitoring her phone and gave my number to John."

"Oh, no, that's terrible. I know she's not the most lovable person in the world, but who would want to hurt an old lady like that? You don't suspect Peter Womack got out of prison somehow? His attempt to kill Alex during the Wolf Ceremony tells me it wouldn't phase him to hurt Minnie either."

"No, that's the first thing everyone thought of. He's still locked up tight as a drum and not going anywhere for a long time. John said that Minnie went to Oklahoma to visit some family members about a month ago and that she'd been acting strange ever since. Said she'd asked him to take her to several different places to pick herbs that she needed for a special assignment."

"That doesn't sound too unusual to me. Everybody knows she keeps lots of herbs and potions around all the time. Wonder what the special assignment was?"

"That's just it—no one knows. John contacted the tribe members in Oklahoma, but they couldn't help much either. The only strange occurrence was that an elder of the tribe passed away while Minnie was there—she was with him at the time. Big Elk was a distant cousin of hers and also a healer. They'd spent a lot of time together prior to his death, he passing on information previously known only to him. Said he didn't trust anyone else besides Minnie with this information."

"Did John say what that was?"

"No, but he suspects it has something to do with her disappearance. Anyway, John is grasping at straws now and wanted me to be aware of what had taken place just in case Minnie shows up or tries to make contact. Since she feels a strong spiritual connection to the Yegua, he thought she might come out to your place."

"And, of course, she wouldn't think about leaving a note behind for her family —that would be too easy. That is, if she's alive."

"Well, to tell the truth, I don't think she's with the departed. Minnie may be small in body, but there's nothing small about her mind. I'm pretty certain she left on her own volition unless........"

"Unless what?"

"What if the information given to her by Big Elk would be of importance to another member of the tribe? Maybe her own tribe kidnapped her. John is afraid someone picked her up while she was on one of her herb forages, and that's a possibility, but I'm more inclined to think this is connected to that trip to Oklahoma."

***

Later that day, I was greeted by Cooter as I came up the driveway and parked the car. We'd become best friends ever since the night he was mauled by the panther. As I opened the car door, I scratched him behind the ears and said, "Cooter, you're still the ugliest dog I've ever seen, but I do believe you're the most lovable one I've ever had the privilege of knowing. Hang, on, buddy, and I'll get you a treat."

Cooter sat down on the cement under the carport and slobbered delightedly all over the doggie treat I'd given him. His shaggy tail beat a syncopated rhythm on the pavement as I made several trips into the house with my purchases from the mall. The splint on his leg had seen better days. It was raggedy and covered in dirt from dragging it along behind him. He seemed to be mending well, though, and Alfons said the splint could come off soon.

My mind still on Minnie, I changed clothes and went outside to work in my flowerbeds before it got too dark to see what I was doing. I noticed that Sandra and her family hadn't gotten home from school, and it was then I remembered they had said they were going to do some shopping and wouldn't be home til later.

It was times like this that it felt lonely out here, and I was glad Cooter was around even if he couldn't talk. Definitely a good idea to marry Burton sooner than later, too. The months I lived out here alone after Heb died taught me that I don't make a very good hermit. Life is meant to be shared, not lived in isolation.

Burton..........the thought of him reminded me why I was outside this evening-- cleaning out flowerbeds and getting things ready for our wedding. Had a nice sound to it. We'd decided to marry at Thanksgiving since both of our families could be here at that time. The gazebo would be the center focus, but I wanted to plant some new chrysanthemums all around the back of the cabin for some bright, fall color.

We decided to include all of our immediate family in the ceremony—all except little Hadyn who was still too young to be a part. A small, private ceremony was what Burton and I both wanted—just our families and closest friends. The reception would be held here as well—a barbeque that we decided to have catered.

As these thoughts occupied my mind, I noticed Cooter's ears at attention as he hopped toward the Yegua. Thinking the panther might have returned, I called,

"Here, Cooter, here, boy. Come on back to the house, now. Nothin' you need to be chasin' out there this evening." Since he didn't respond, I hustled out to where he was, picked him up, and took him inside the house with me.

My heart was racing from exertion and fear as I remembered the panther's awful scream from the other night—and Cooter's fight with death. I closed and locked all the doors and pulled the blinds.

Something, or someone was out there. I could feel it. Hopefully, Sandra and Jack would be home soon. As a precaution, I went to the closet and got Heb's old shotgun off the gun rack. I set it beside the fireplace and went about fixing something to eat for Cooter and myself.

***

After our meal, Cooter and I went into the den where I turned on the TV and sat in the recliner. The evening was cool, so I pulled a comforter around my legs for warmth. Cooter sat at the foot of the chair with pleading eyes that said, "Please let me sit in your lap—just this once."

"No, no, we're not gonna start that, I began," but one more look into those limpid eyes was all it took. "I can't believe I'm doing this," I heard myself say as I bent over and picked up that mangy little dog.

I must've fallen asleep because Cooter's little ruff-ruff growl startled me. His ever-alert ears heard Jack's pickup coming up the road long before I could even see the headlights.

Soon, the kids were home and headed this way.

"Nana, Nana," I heard Emma yelling as Cooter ran for the door barking loudly.

When the door opened, two excited little girls fell inside and into Cooter's slobbery embrace. "Cooter! We was worried 'bout you," cried Kassie.

After Jack and Sandra got inside, I told them about our experience and Jack quickly said, "We'll need to keep Cooter inside at night from now on. He's simply too small to hold his own against a panther or a wolf. I'll feel a lot better with him indoors."

"I think that's a good idea, Jack," added Sandra, "but he's not sleeping with the girls. He can sleep on that old comforter by the fireplace."

"Awwwwwww, Mom!" conspired Emma and Kassie who cautiously exchanged a secret glance.

I wondered how long those sleeping arrangements would last. When it came to denying Cooter, it was a loosing battle.

Jack and Sandra had no idea that there was no real wolf—only a panther to contend with, but again, what could I say? They wouldn't believe me anyway, so I just let it go.

***

After a drive into Lexington to the greenhouse the next morning, I came home with the Ranger loaded down with fall plants and some stepping stones from Woodson Lumber.I planned to make a rock path from the patio to the gazebo for the wedding party so our shoes would stay clean during the ceremony.

As I unloaded the truck, my phone rang. It was Burton. "Joan, I've just had a call from John Williams and he thinks that Minnie has been back to her house."

"Why on earth does he think that?" I blurted out.

"Some things are missing that would be of importance only to her. He said she always kept some special little pots used for mixing herbs on the window sill above the sink. Those were missing and he knew he'd seen them a day or so ago. Also, two worn, leather pouches she'd brought back from Oklahoma were gone. She'd hung them on a nail on the side of her pantry.

The crazy thing is that no one saw her come or go, and there are no footprints anywhere. It's almost as if Minnie has become part of the spirit world that she so often is in tune with. If that's happened, we may never see her again."

"Burton, maybe she has to finish this quest, this assignment given her by her cousin before she can return. As much as I hate getting involved in another Indian affair, I would do anything to help Minnie."

"The million dollar question, though, is what could we possibly do to help her? If her own son doesn't know what to do, what makes you think we can help?"

"Burton, I think that Minnie is the wolf I saw out in the pasture the other day. She stared at me like we'd met before. I can't explain it, but somehow, I think it was her."

"Could be, Joan, but even if it is her, I don't have a clue as to how to help her and there's always the possibility that she doesn't want or need our help."

"Her connection to this area is very strong, Burton. I just know it's her and I'm going to do my best to find out before our wedding. I don't want to have to worry about all that hocus-pocus while we're saying our vows!"

***

Burton arrived at my house late Friday evening after work. He had brought a load of his personal things and would spend the weekend. He wanted to help me get the yard ready for the wedding as well as spend some time thinking about Minnie's disappearance.

Even though it was dark and cool, we decided to take a couple of lawn chairs down to the creek and make a fire. The Yegua flowed freely now after the recent rains. I always enjoyed sitting close to her. She had a soothing effect on me. Sometimes she told me things— things from the past, snippets quietly whispered into my ears.

Tonight her voice was calling me…faintly telling me…. Suddenly Burton broke the spell, "Joan, are you alright? You're acting a little strange."

His broad hand reached out and pushed a strand of disheveled hair from my eyes as I jumped up and looked around. Who had just spoken to me? No one was there besides Burton, and that certainly wasn't Burton's voice I had heard beckoning me.

I stared at him in disbelief as the voice weakened and drifted away with the creek's water. "Did you hear that?" I exclaimed.

"Hear what, Hon?"

"I'm not sure, but someone was calling my name. Minnie's in trouble and we have to help her. We need to go to the bridge. Don't ask me why, I just know we need to go right now. Hurry!"

***

Quickly, we gathered up flashlights, guns, and our cell phones and jumped into my Ranger. Since I knew the lay-out of the field better than Burton, I drove. Burton's tall frame hit the top of the cab more than once as we bounced across bumps in the road. "Sorry," was all I had time to say as I raced toward the bridge.

Soon we'd passed the tank dam and were headed downhill toward the broken bridge where I'd last seen the wolf. The truck's headlights were on high-beam, but I wished for even more light on this dark, eerie night. Mist had crept up from the bottom land and covered the windshield. I had to turn on the wipers just to see where we were going.

"Slow down, Joan, or we'll end up in the ravine!" Burton yelled over the chaos and noise. I took a quick peek over at him and realized he was about as scared as I was. He had a white-knuckle grip on the "Oh, shit" handle and was vigorously wiping moisture from the window with his other hand.

No sooner than I had looked away, my attention was drawn back to the road.

The bridge was looming up before us and this time it was Burton who saw it. "There! There! She's sitting on the bridge!"

There was no need to ask. I knew who was sitting on the bridge, and as we approached, she turned into a little, white cloud that blended into the water vapor floating across the pasture. Just like that—gone.

The Ranger came to a halt just a few yards shy of the bridge as Burton and I both opened our doors and got out. It's hard to describe what we felt at that moment. We were exhilarated, scared and anxious all at the same time. Dealing with the spirit world was still strange to us, and knowing that Minnie was somehow mixed up in all of this made us desperate as well.

Burton walked toward the spot on the bridge where we'd seen the wolf. I knew that sensation. One second there's a physical being present and a nano-second later it vanishes into thin air. Our human brains simply cannot wrap themselves around this phenomenon—it just doesn't compute.

As I was about to speak, Burton bent down and picked up something on the bridge near the spot where the wolf had been. Slowly, deliberately, he strode back to the truck and held out his hand. In the dim light, I could make out a small, leather pouch.

"Do you suppose........?" I began as Burton opened the pouch. He poured out the contents into his hand--a piece of horn, a dried beetle and some leaves.

"Yes, it was Minnie, he offered. This must be one of the missing pouches from her house. I think she is giving us information the only way she can at this time. I'll contact John and tell him what's going on. Maybe he'll know what this means."

Chapter Five

Cooter met my truck as I pulled up to the barn behind the cabin. "Not now, Cooter, we've got some important business to attend to and, besides, you're supposed to be inside your own house after dark. Get home."

Dejectedly, Cooter hopped back home as Sandra's porch light came on. "Is everything alright, Mom? I saw you out in the pasture......"

"Everything's fine, Sandra, Burton's with me. We just took a little joy-ride, that's all," I lied.

"Okay, Mom, 'night," she yelled as Cooter ran past her legs and into the security of his newly-found home.

Collecting all our paraphernalia, we headed for the cabin. Not wasted on our ears was the echoing call of a lone wolf. I instinctively grabbed Burton's hand and held on tightly all the way to the back door.

Once inside, we again examined the contents of what we believed to be Minnie's herb pouch: a broken horn, a dried beetle and some sort of leaves. What could she possibly be trying to tell us? It was late, but we felt we had to call John and tell him what we had found.

John's wife answered but quickly handed the phone to her husband. "John here."

"John, this is Burton Mosley. I'm out at Joan's place on the Yegua, and we think we have made contact with your mother."

After a brief explanation, John said, "I'm really not surprised. When I discovered her things missing from the kitchen, I knew she was still alive. She has acted strangely, even for her, ever since her trip to visit Big Elk in Oklahoma. His death really affected her, but she refused to tell me much of anything concerning him or his request of her. Let me know if anything else happens. I'll get in touch with the elders of the tribe and see if they can shed any light on the situation. Thank's for your help, Burton, you're a good friend."

There was nothing else to do, so after a quick shower and a late-night snack, we headed to bed.

***

Minnie's feet led her back to her own front door. It was good to be upright again. Big Elk's power had been transferred to her upon his death, but she was not a young woman and her back hurt. Changing from one form to another took a lot of energy as well, and she sometimes forgot some of her mentor's last-minute instructions.

No matter. One good thing was that she did not have to worry about sustenance when she was in her "other self". One did not have need of food, water, or sleep, for that matter. That gave Minnie more time to spend on her quest. She knew her time was limited. Soon, she too would join her ancestors in sleep. Big Elk did not finish his mission before he passed away, and he trusted Minnie to complete what he had started. The Tonkawa tribe desperately needed information lost to them many generations ago and Minnie was their last hope—only they did not know this.

Just a few more days and she thought she'd find the answer she so diligently sought. She wished her grandson, Alex, was there. He was young, strong and intelligent. Surely he would help her.

Minnie didn't want to rely on anyone outside the tribe, but Big Elk's instructions were clear—the big professor would be able to complete the task Minnie wouldn't be able to finish on her own. Whatever that was, was still hidden to Minnie, but she knew she was getting closer to the answer every day. She would use the white woman, Joan, to bring Mosley when she needed him. Big Elk said the professor would be given the knowledge to help her from the three clues. Good thing she could still hear some of Big Elk's whisperings—even though death separated them for awhile.

***

When I woke up the next day, Burton was already in the kitchen with a pot of coffee brewing. The cabin was cold, so I put on my faded flannel bathrobe and fuzzy houseshoes. After a quick trip to the bathroom to splash my face and brush my unruly hair, I made my way to the kitchen.

"Mornin', Sunshine, you don't look too chipper this morning. What's wrong?"

"Good morning to you, too," I chattered. "I'm glad you've got that coffee ready, it's freezing in here."

"Do you want a fire, or should I turn up the thermostat?"

"Thermostat—too cold to wait on the fireplace! Brrrrrr!!!"

After blueberry pancakes and another cup of coffee, I began to thaw out. Burton sat at the table lingering between the morning paper and Minnie's three clues. The strange items sat side-by-side on the frosty window sill next to Burton's pipe and bag of tobacco.

After a long silence, he ventured, "I'm 99% sure the broken horn is from an elk and that would give reference to Big Elk, Minnie's cousin, but the beetle and the leaves are still a mystery. I won't rest until I figure this out, Joan, so if you don't mind, I'm going to head to my office at the University. There are some books there that may give me a lead. After that, I think I'll pay a call to John Williams and show him the pouch. If this isn't Minnie's pouch, we could be barking up the wrong tree."

"Oh, Burton, I know how important this is, but I was hoping we could spend the day together and finalize our wedding and honeymoon plans. Besides, I still need some help with the yard work and the wedding is only three weeks away." I put on my most pathetic look and cozied up into his lap, morning breath and all.

Feeling rather frisky, Burton brushed his stubby beard all over the back of my neck and began goosing me on my ticklish left side. He encapsulated me in a bear-hug and squeezed tight. "Okay, okay, I give!" as I escaped to the opposite side of the table.

With the threat of continued torment written all over his face, Burton began to rise from his seat. Finally, with his goofy professor grin, he claimed victory and sat back down.

"Now, you were saying………." he went on.

"I was just saying that I could use your help around here this weekend. If you will lay the rocks on the pathway to the gazebo, I'll finish up the flowerbeds. Deal?"

"Deal. As soon as I get back from Austin, I'm all yours, I promise."

***

Burton pored over a number of texts, some of them ancient, and finally came to the conclusion that what he had on his desk besides an elk horn was a dried scarab beetle, also known as the dung beetle, and some mesquite leaves.

It appeared that some early Indian tribes thought the scarab beetle had a mystic connection to the sun, but a sure fact was that those same beetles had often rolled up marble-sized balls of buffalo dung. That in itself wasn't hard to visualize since ranches all over Texas still have dung beetles working their pastures.

Burton had to search a little harder to find a connection to the mesquite leaves. What could Minnie be trying to tell him about a mesquite tree? True, there were several large mesquites in Joan's pasture, but if they held any importance, he didn't see it.

Finally, after some searching on the internet, Burton discovered that native Indians used mesquite flour made from the tree's bean pods. They also chewed the pods which tasted somewhat like honey. One medicinal fact that may have been of interest to Minnie as a healer, was that a diet rich in mesquite almost obliterated diabetes from Indians living in the southwest part of the U.S.

After quickly jotting down some notes, Burton locked up his office and drove over to John William's office on the northeast side of town. He hoped John wouldn't mind the intrusion, but he felt he was on to something. Besides, he needed John to positively identify the leather pouch as Minnie's.

Soon Burton stood face-to-face with John in his office. John turned the pouch over and over in his hand before emptying out its contents. "Yes, I am certain this is my mother's pouch," he claimed. "I distinctly remember the small, red markings around the drawstring."

"John, do you have any insights about the horn, beetle or leaves?" asked Burton.

"I am sure you already know that the broken horn came from an elk, so I would assume that's a reference to our cousin, Big Elk. What kind of leaves are these?"

"I'm 95% sure they're from a mesquite. Since they grow all over

Central Texas, they're nothing extraordinary. Seems your people made flour from the mesquite bean which kept diabetes at bay."

"Diabetes? I was told that Big Elk died from complications of diabetes. Burton, you may be on to something here. If Big Elk sent my mother on a quest, she will die before she comes back without an answer, and frankly, I'm not ready to let her go. What can I do to help you find her?"

"I'm not sure at this point, but talk to your tribe again. See if they can shed some more light on this diabetes issue. I have a gut feeling that's at the bottom of this whole situation."

***

Soiled and tired from yard work, I took a break. To tell the truth, I was a little miffed that Burton still had not come home. The afternoon sun had warmed me to the point that sweat was popping up on my forehead, so I decided to take my tea down to the fish pond and sit in the shade of the ancient live oak beside it.

From that vantage point, I surveyed the back yard making a mental note to find a few Mexican Heather bushes to fill in some blank spots around the gazebo. After all, I wasn't getting married but once more in my lifetime and I did want things to look nice. We had hired a professional photographer and most of our photos would be shot in or around the gazebo.

It was there at the pond that Burton found me when he drove up a few minutes later."Hey, Hon, sorry I'm late…" he started.

The sight of my intended's rugged face drove away all thoughts of self-pity, so I smiled up at him and gave him my hand. He pulled me up and planted a big, ole syrupy kiss right between my eyes. "Yuck!" I said pretending to be offended.

"Wow, you've been busy since this morning. I can't believe you've gotten so much done. Sorry I'm late, but I think I've made some real headway on Minnie's disappearance."

Together, we walked to the patio and sat down in the recliners as Burton continued. "I've come to the conclusion that Minnie is working on a project that has something to do with diabetes. John told me that Big Elk died from diabetes complications. The leaves in the pouch were from a mesquite tree, and in my research this morning, I discovered that the Indians used to make flour from the tree's bean pods. Apparently, a diet rich in mesquite greatly reduced the occurrence of the disease, which the natives were prone to have."

"That's amazing, but why on earth is Minnie haunting us in the form of a wolf ?"

"I'm not sure what she's looking for, but apparently she needs to travel to another dimension or time, and we already know that the wolf represents her people. So, my guess is that she needs to contact someone or find something from the tribe's past. Whatever she is searching for is surely located here on the Yegua, and it looks like her destiny is in our hands whether we like it or not."

***

For the rest of the afternoon, Burton and I worked side-by-side laying the rocks to the gazebo. Mostly, we worked in silence, enjoying the warm autumn afternoon. Our eyes often met in quiet reassurance of the companionship and love we shared. I no longer sought Heb's approval or needed it. I knew I'd made the right decision.

Kassie and Emma played nearby with Cooter, who was now free of his cast. They happily threw sticks for him to chase and squealed with delight if he actually caught one mid-air.

Sandra soon joined all of us with a pitcher of lemonade and some glasses, so we all went to the gazebo and sat down for a much-needed rest.

"Everything is really looking nice, Mom. I'm sorry I haven't been much help, but just getting caught up on the laundry on the weekends is about all I can handle these days. However, I would like to fix supper for all of us tonight, so whatta 'ya say?"

Before I could open my mouth, Burton answered for me. "I can't think of anyone else I'd rather eat with tonight!" As he said this, he grabbed all three of my girls until they begged to be released. Kassie and Emma ran screaming out of the gazebo with Burton close on their heels.

Sandra and I amusedly watched as the girls dodged around trees, shrubs and fence posts to avoid being caught by their new "grandpa". Being the youngest, Kassie was captured first and was soon dangling over the fish pond. "No, no, no," she screamed not meaning a word of it. And, with great ease and care, Burton lowered her into the water up to her knees. She kicked water all over him before Emma joined in the fracas.

Pretty soon, all three were soaking wet, laughing and rolling on the ground. "Looks like your laundry load just got a little bigger, Sandra," I said.

"Well, they were dirty anyway so guess it won't matter too much. I'm just glad they've accepted Burton so easily after Dad's passing. And, I want you to know that I couldn't be happier for you. I see how much joy Burton's brought into your life and he has come to hold a special place in our hearts as well."

"Thank you, for sharing that with me. I can't wait 'til we're married and he can be here all the time. But, for now, tell me what I can help you with for supper."

"How 'bout you do a salad? Since it's such a gorgeous day, why don't we eat out on your patio? Say, 6 o'clock?"

***

Later that evening, Sandra, Jack, the girls and Cooter all strolled over to my cabin laden with bowls and platters of food which were placed inside. After filling our plates and glasses, we went outside and sat on the big picnic table Alfons had built the year before.

Heads bowed, we thanked the Good Lord for our wonderful meal and the day's blessings.

Finishing first, Jack put down his plate and gathered some wood for the patio fire pit. I went inside for some hot chocolate and cookies. The evening could not have been more pleasant—no panther, no howling wolves, no interruptions. We talked late into the night discussing cattle, wedding plans, school, the upcoming holidays....

Darkness continued to seep in around us as, one-by-one, we began to yawn. Emma and Kassie soon lay limp in their parents' laps while Cooter snored under the table. Once again, life was good on the Yegua.

Chapter Six

BURTON LEFT NOT LONG AFTER breakfast on Monday morning. We had finished all but the last yard or so of the rock pathway to the gazebo on Sunday afternoon, so I decided to complete that on my own while he was gone. After washing the last of the breakfast dishes, I put on my jacket and headed outside.

Carefully, I rolled my old rusty wheelbarrow down to the gazebo. The path was winding, so was quite lengthy and had taken more rocks than we'd originally thought. In reality though, it wasn't such a hard project, given the fact the soil was mostly sandy in this part of the yard.

The Yegua bottomland had come back to life after the fall rains. It was a pleasure to be outside working in the cool air, so I didn't mind the exertion from lifting and laying the rocks in a hap-hazard pattern. As I labored, my mind drifted to our upcoming nuptials.

Sandra and I had finished the last of the wedding invitations the day before, so I made a mental note to get them in the mailbox before the mail truck made its afternoon rounds. There weren't that many to be sent, besides, everyone had already been contacted by phone at least once.

The only close family member we weren't sure would make it was

Burton's son, Michael, who was still in the Air Force. His oldest son, Sean, planned on driving down and bringing his fiancé, Amy, with him. This would be the first time for us to meet her, so we looked forward to that as well.

We tried hard to keep the guest list small, but it seemed to grow day by day. Oh well, there was plenty of room in the yard, and if it rained we'd just hustle everyone over to the little church up the road. I'd already reserved it in case of an emergency, and Pastor Fettke had been forewarned.

As wedding thoughts continued to dance around my mind, I cleared the space for the last rock. As a surprise for Burton, I'd had a large stone engraved with our names and wedding date. Jack had hidden it in the barn for me and covered it with hay to keep Burton from finding it earlier. It would be the landing stone for the gazebo. After laying it in place, I stood back to admire it—perfect!

***

After a light lunch, I decided to take a book to the gazebo and do some reading. The day had remained pleasant and I wanted to take advantage of the beautiful weather while I could. Stepping out of my shoes, I mindlessly kicked sand off the rocks while walking the entire path for the first time. Childhood rhymes teased my mind as I went from stone to stone, "One-two, buckle my shoe, three-four, shut the door...."

Cooter drifted over from his yard, expecting a hand-out as usual. I often kept treats in my pocket to reward the little mutt. He had gained weight and now sported a shiny coat of fur. His limp was almost gone, for which I was grateful. Bless his heart, he was almost handsome after a few weeks of tender loving care from Sandra and the girls.

As my foot reached the last step, my lighthearted mood was immediately extinguished. Our matrimony rock was completely covered with sand. Instinctively, I looked around for the intruder, but could not see man or beast anywhere. Checking the surrounding area for footprints, I found none other than my own and Cooter's. Surely he would have warned me if there'd been someone in the yard—he always barked when someone approached the property. But there he sat in total oblivion, chewing on the rawhide bone I'd given him.

Shaking my head, puzzled and wary, I entered the gazebo. No sooner than I sat down to read, something caught the corner of my eye. Hanging on a nail just inside the entry was another leather pouch. It was identical to the one left on the bridge earlier—red markings and all. Minnie had made another appearance.

"Where are you?" I yelled into the quietness of the yard. "Why won't you just come and ask for help, and why do you insist on these insipid clues instead of simply telling us what you need?" Poor Cooter, who thought I was yelling at him, looked at me warily and moved to the shade of a nearby tree to continue chewing his bone in peace.

After my short-lived temper-tantrum, I finally remembered that wolves don't write notes or talk, even though my grandson had earlier said Lobo spoke to him "in his head". If Minnie wanted help from Burton and me, she must be desperate and was communicating the only way she could. With this realization, my anger abated and I removed the bag from the nail.

Gingerly, I untied the leather strings and opened the pouch. Fearful of what could be inside, I dumped the contents onto the gazebo floor. Cold chills ran up my spine when I saw what lay there. Within seconds, Burton's cell phone was ringing.

***

I ran into the cabin immediately upon viewing the horrible "thing" lying on the floor. Fearing Cooter would tamper with the "evidence", I picked him up and took him inside with me. He began whining and scratching the back door to be let out. "Cooter, stop that and hush up! You aren't going back outside for awhile, so settle down."

Burton wasn't able to get to the cabin for another two incredibly long, hours. It seemed an eternity before Cooter's "Woof-woof" announced his approach. Thankful he'd come, I ran outside to greet him and take him out back to see what I'd discovered in Minnie's bag.

As we approached the gazebo, I noticed that the sand had blown off of our special rock. Burton was pleased to see it of course, but I was in shock-- the wedding date had miraculously been changed. "I know for a fact this stone said November 25th, and now it says the 24th—Thanksgiving Day! How can that be?"

Before we could wrap our minds around that phenomenon, Burton stepped into the gazebo to stare at the dropped pouch and its contents. Behind us, a dark shadow suddenly lunged forward, but Burton was quicker. "No, boy, this is not something you want to eat, believe me!" A disappointed Cooter ducked his head and retreated to the blanket on his own back porch as Burton picked up the disgusting body part and turned it around and around in his hand.

After a thorough examination, he dropped the offensive thing back into the pouch and nonchalantly said, "Well, I'll be dadgummed, it's a mummified ear."

"That's all you can say? It's some person's EAR, not just an arrowhead or a broken piece of pottery, or a moccasin, or, or........"

"Joan, you forget that I handle this sort of thing every day in my line of work. It's not that big of a deal."

"Maybe not to you, but it's not every day that an ear is sitting in my gazebo and I know that the wedding date on the landing stone was changed. What I don't know is why and how."

As my hysteria subsided, we retraced our steps back to the cabin. As we entered, Burton softly tossed the offensive pouch on the table.

"No," I screamed, "get that thing off of my table and OUT of my house!"

He quickly put the pouch in his front pocket and calmly said, "Sure thing, I'll take it with me when I go."

"No, no, you don't understand. I want it out NOW. The thought of that obnoxious thing inside my house, much less on my table, gives me the creeps. Please, take it out now!"

"Okay, okay, I'll go put it in my truck. So, what's for supper?"

"How can you even think about food after holding that thing?" I questioned.

"I don't know. Guess it just doesn't have the same affect on me, that's all."

Burton realized I meant what I said and knew that if he wanted supper, he'd best get a move on. Soon, the "ear" rested on the seat of his truck, and my pulse went back to normal.

***

I insisted Burton scrub his hands thoroughly before sitting down at the table, which had already been sanitized. I fixed him a glass of tea and we talked while I put together some sandwiches.

"Minnie must be getting really desperate to have left that despicable thing for me to find," I muttered.

"That's kinda what I'm thinkin' myself, Joan. I'll get back in touch with John and run today's events by him. Maybe he'll see something we don't. One thing's for sure though, that ear is well over a hundred years old. Wouldn't be surprised if it wasn't left over from the early 1800's. I'm just wondering how Minnie came by it?"

We took our sandwiches to the table and devoured them in no

57

time. Burton offered to clean up, so I let him while I munched on some cookies the girls had brought over the day before. Afterwards, we went outside and built a fire on the patio.

"I know Minnie is only trying to help her people, but it would be nice if I didn't have to be scared half out of my wits each time there's a crisis," I grumbled, "and her timing couldn't be worse. Last year, it was the Thanksgiving holidays and this year it's our wedding that's being interrupted!"

"Well, Joan, if you'll remember correctly, these Indian "problems" are what brought us together in the first place. I, for one, am not complaining, but I do realize it's been frightful for you at times. Maybe this mystery will be solved soon and we won't have to deal with any more problems concerning Minnie and her tribe."

That said, Burton filled and lit his pipe, adding to the pleasant aroma rising from the fire pit. Realizing that what he'd said was true, I soon calmed down and began to enjoy the evening. We pulled our recliners side-by-side to share a downy comforter as the moon shed her golden beams over the yard. Silently, a trophy buck leapt across the Yegua and wandered over to the feeder on our side of the creek. The day slowly closed its curtain to the sound of dueling nightingales, and I gently lay my sleepy head on Burton's shoulder.

Soon the lights in Jack and Sandra's house went out, but we were reluctant to move. The moon's eerie light and the Yegua's gurgling song had worked together to weave a magic web over us. Like fodder for a spider, we were held tightly in its grip, and sleep soon overcame our tired bodies.

Some time later, Burton shook me awake. "Sunshine, I don't know what came over us, but it's freezing out here, let's get inside."

Arthritis claimed the real victory, though, as we both painfully hobbled into the cabin.

***

When I woke the next morning, Burton was gone. He'd left a note for me on the kitchen table. It read, "Didn't want to wake you. Have an early class today. Will call later. Have a great day. Love you, B."

Groggily, I made myself some coffee and sat down at the table. Burton's cold pipe lay in an ashtray in the windowsill. I inhaled the cherry-flavored scent that reminded me so of him and re-read his note. "Love you, B." It made me smile just to read that simple phrase.

Soon he would be living at the cabin 24/7 and I couldn't wait for that time to come. Many of his belongings had already been brought out here and it gave me comfort to see his boots by the back door, his reading glasses on the end table, and his leather jacket hanging on the coat rack.

There were definitely no lingering doubts about marrying this man—quite the opposite. Now, my biggest fear was that something would happen to prevent my marrying Burton.

***

After morning classes were done, Burton made a quick call to John Williams asking him to come over to his office at UT. John promised to be there shortly after his lunch break, but was running late.

"Mother, I have no idea what kind of trouble you've gotten yourself into," he thought to himself, "but I do know this—I will be glad when you're safely home and are done with whatever it is Big Elk has asked you to do. If you would just learn to trust me, maybe I wouldn't have to worry about you so much."

Soon John's BMW was parked in front of the anthropology building and he was running up the stairs. He hated being late, but the traffic in Austin was always unpredictable.

Burton's secretary led John down the hall to his office. "Dr. Mosley, Mr. Williams is here. Do you need anything else before I leave? My class starts in fifteen minutes, so I'd better get going."

"Just mail those letters on your way out, that's all. Thanks."

Standing up, Burton greeted his visitor, "John, good to see you again."

"Same here. Sorry I'm late, but you know how the traffic is around here. Stupidly left my cell phone in the office or I would've called. Anyway, I'm not too sure I want to hear what you have to tell me."

"Well, maybe you do. Minnie has been back to Joan's place and left this behind. I'm sure you'll agree it's a match to the first pouch left on the bridge by the wolf— your mother. We know she's still alive, but we think she's encountered a situation that she can't handle by herself. Look inside and see what you think."

John quickly opened the sac and dropped it on the floor. "Damn, Mosley, you coulda warned me!"

"Sorry........I'm around this kind of thing all the time and forget the effect it has on some people."

"Somehow, I doubt that…. but oddly enough, I think… I know what this is."

"Care to share that information, or is it 'need-to-know' only?"

"Well, when I was a boy, our family would go to tribal meetings once a year in Oklahoma. On one of these trips, our cousins told my older sister a story about a shaman's ear, which she related to me just to scare me. I suppose I sort've half-believed it back then, but was afraid to mention it to our parents for fear of reprisal. We were not allowed to speak of such things, and until now I had forgotten about the story—thought it was only a myth."

"Go on……."

"It seems that we have an ancestor, went by the Spanish name of El Mocho, who was a tribal medicine man in the early 1800's. He was very powerful—the most powerful of all the shamans known before. When it came near the time for him to join his ancestors in sleep, he passed on his knowledge to the "chosen one". As he lay dying, he asked for a sharp knife to be brought to him. With only the apprentice as a witness, El Mocho took the knife, quickly sliced off his ear, and handed it to the man. With his dying words, he said the ear would bring special knowledge and power to the person possessing it—would allow them to hear him speaking from the after-life."

"….and, the ear has been passed down all these years from one shaman to another--so Big Elk gave it to Minnie before he died."

"Apparently."

"That would mean that she will pass it down to your son, Alex, then?"

"I would assume so."

"John, why don't you take this, ah, this specimen to Alex. Maybe he has received enough training from Minnie to help her now. Maybe that's what she's been waiting for."

"You'd think she would just give the ear to him herself if she needed help from Alex. There must be some other reason why she is channeling things through you and Joan."

"I thought of that also. Maybe College Station is too far away. Minnie is old and may be getting weak. Is Alex coming home any time soon?"

"I'll call him tonight and make sure he's here this weekend. When I explain to him that his Maw-maw needs his help, he'll be here. I've seen a lot of my mother in him, and after watching him at the Wolf Dance last year, I feel he has more power than even he knows of."

Chapter Seven

"WHAT DID YOU SAY? YOU have to speak louder, my cousin, for my ears are old."

Unknown to her family, Minnie had spent the night in her own bed. She'd been careful not to turn on any lights to evade being found. If they interrupted her schedule, she may never find the secret to help her tribe. Many relatives had already died an untimely death, with others sure to follow. Hadn't Big Elk died too soon? She felt sure he had at least twelve more moons left before joining their ancestors in sleep. Her medicine had failed to help him, and without the ancient ingredients and dosage, she would not be able to help others.

Alex was next in line to inherit her tribe's special powers, but he was behind in his training due to his attending A&M University in College Station. John had insisted Alex get a degree in business, but Alex chose medicine instead. Maybe that was a good thing, but Minnie hadn't seen him since he left in late August. If only she could summon Alex home this weekend.......before it was too late. Her own powers were weakening.

But, for now, she needed to concentrate on Big Elk's whispers. His voice was not strong, but he pled for justice from the grave. What was he trying to tell her? Maybe she should not have left the ear for the white woman to find, but that insured her Mosley would get involved. She and Alex would need his help later on.

***

Black Tooth tossed restlessly in his bed. For the past couple of weeks he had not slept, and sweat trickled across his wrinkled brow. Big Elk's face tormented him nightly, robbing him of sweet sleep. He was not a young man any more—he needed his rest.

Black Tooth glanced over at his fat wife snoring beside him. He resented the fact she could sleep so soundly when he could not. Not only could he not sleep, he found that food did not satisfy him any more. His wife was an excellent cook, but now her food was bitter in his mouth. Soon he would be half the size of his wife and she would lose respect for him. Did he not have trouble from her already? She often turned him down when he tried to make love to her. He couldn't remember the last time she even smiled at him. She went her own way and did whatever she wanted instead of what he wanted.

It was Big Elk's fault he had so many troubles and his wife now despised him. Big Elk should have been teaching him tribal secrets instead of that old hag cousin of his. Minnie was almost as old as Big Elk anyway. What was the point in that?

Good thing he ended Big Elk's life before he told Minnie everything he knew. No one suspected he'd been poisoning Big Elk all along--just a few drops in his food every now and then. Black Tooth's wife, Nancy, had often asked him to take food over to Big Elk, and he was glad to oblige. Everyone knew Big Elk had trouble with diabetes and would assume that's what killed him. Indians didn't believe in modern autopsies, so he had nothing to worry about—no one would know, and as next of kin, he inherited the house and Big Elk's Caddie. Now all he had to do was go through Big Elk's belongings. Surely he would find something to help him gain power with his people. If El Mocho's sacred ear really existed, he'd find it-- unless that fool had already given it to Minnie.

But, Black Tooth had forgotten one important thing. Big Elk's powers went beyond the grave—with or without the sacred talisman.

***

Alex, John, and Burton met secretly at John's office the following Saturday. Unknown to them, Minnie was there as well. She rather enjoyed this new-found power given to her by Big Elk.

"Hello, Burton. You remember my son, Alex?"

"Of course. Who could forget the main attraction at the Wolf Dance last year? How is school going?"

"Fine, Dr. Mosley. I hope you don't hold it against me that I went to A&M instead of UT?"

"Not at all, young man. I happen to be an A&M grad myself. I generally keep that under my hat as you can well imagine. An Aggie teaching at UT is subject to quite a bit of ridicule. But, enough about me, I understand you're studying medicine at A&M?"

"Yes, sir, that's correct. My grandmother has instilled a passion for healing in me, and I feel that's where I can best serve my people."

"Excellent! Has your father told you why we brought you here today?"

"Sort of. I know it has something to do with my grandmother, and that she's been missing for a couple of weeks now. My parents had not told me about her disappearance. They didn't want me to worry—to stay focused on my studies. But, somehow I felt there was trouble. I dreamed about her the other night and she seemed to be calling to me."

"John, do you want to show him the bag now?"

At this suggestion, John pulled Minnie's bag from his desk drawer and laid it out within Alex's reach. Alex instinctively put his hand out to take the pouch, but his father stopped him. "Son, this is one of the pouches your grandmother brought home with her from Oklahoma. Are you familiar with our elderly cousin Big Elk?"

"Yes, father. I know he was the tribal healer and that Maw-maw went to see him before he passed away. He was supposed to give her some last-minute training since she was the one chosen to inherit his powers."

"Alex, has your grandmother ever told you that you were to inherit these same powers or, gifts?" inquired Burton.

"Yes,sir. She has told me that ever since I can remember. She often called me to come to her house so she could teach me to identify herbs and mix potions. I suppose that's why I've always had a close connection to her, but I also see the need to study medicine formally, to be better informed, to help my people—all people."

"Son, I want you to be prepared for what you will see inside this bag before I open it," said John. "I'll have to admit that it took me by surprise when Dr. Mosley handed it to me."

Having said that, John emptied the pouch onto his desk and watched his son's face intently. Burton, too, focused on Alex as he gingerly picked up the sacred ear and studied it. "El Mocho's ear..."Suddenly, all three of them were aware of an unseen energy in the room and Alex said, "She's here. Maw-maw Singing Bird is here........"

Silence filled the little office as Alex's dark eyes glazed over and drooped shut. His dark head slumped on his chest, breathing so slight as to cause concern. John and Burton exchanged unsure glances as they eased Alex into a chair and waited for him to awaken. One, two, three, and finally ten minutes passed with no sound being heard except for the always present whir of traffic in the street below.

Periodically, Alex' head would rise and he would grasp at some imaginary thing or being.

Finally, his eyes popped open and he stared at the shriveled body part in his hand. His hand began to shake uncontrollably as he struggled to put El Mocho's ear back in the pouch. As if he now knew his purpose, Alex looped the pouch over his head to hang around his neck.

Looking at his father, Alex simply stated, "We will meet with my grandmother tonight. She wants us to come to the bridge on Ms. Johnston's property.

Then turning to Burton, he said, "Dr. Mosley, you know where this is?"

"Yes, of course! I'll take you there."

***

My phone rang shortly after that secluded meeting. "Hello, Burton, where are you? I hadn't heard from you today and I was worried."

"I'm sorry, Joan, but I had some unfinished business with John and Alex Williams this morning. I'll explain later, but we all need to come out to your place tonight and drive down to the bridge where we last saw Minnie. Is that okay with you?"

"I guess so, Burton. Do you think Minnie is alright? Does Alex know what's going on?"

"She seems to be okay for now, but apparently is getting very weak. She, for some reason, used you and me to summon Alex home from school with that mummified ear you found. I guess we'll know more after tonight? You coming along?"

"You know I am. See you soon."

***

With Sandra's family conveniently out of town for the weekend, we had the run of the place to ourselves. John, Alex, and Burton arrived at the cabin just after sundown. They pulled into my driveway in Burton's truck, so I simply crawled into the cab for the journey down to the bridge in the pasture.

Alex got out to open the gate on the new fence Jack had put up between our houses and the stock tank. The cattle had been drinking from the Yegua most of the summer, but the drought had made it necessary for them to come near the house for water, and the fence had been in disrepair.

After rewiring the gate, Alex simply jumped into the truck bed instead of re-entering the cab. Burton carefully drove us through the first pasture and then headed downhill to the ravine. Cattle slept in small groups here and there. They'd never seen Burton's truck before, so they kept a wide berth. We would've been swamped with them begging for corn if we'd come down in my pickup.

Reaching our destination, Burton turned off the engine and we all got out. Alex simply jumped over the side of the pickup, and it was then I noticed Minnie's pouch hanging around his neck. I secretly cringed inside and could not imagine wearing that disgusting thing around my neck. Praying this would be the most disgusting thing I'd see this evening, I followed the men down to the bridge.

The evening was unseasonably cold for November, and there was a fine mist coming down, making it quite miserable. I reached inside my jacket pocket and pulled out a pair of gloves to wear. Not wanting to be a ninny, I hurriedly put them on and ran to catch up with the guys. My glasses kept fogging up, making it hard to see.

Chivalry was definitely dead this unpleasant evening. The three men ahead of me hardly took notice that I struggled to keep up with them. They were men with a mission, and nothing would deter them from their destination.

It was a moonless night, and John was the only one who'd thought to bring a flashlight. Silently, the four of us followed John's puny light beam as we trekked the final fifty yards to the broken bridge. The men finally realized I was not with them and turned to find my hair entangled in some mesquite brush a good 30 feet behind them. Burton came to my rescue and helped me out. "Sorry. Thought you were with us. Why didn't you say something?"

After rescuing my fly-away curls from the mesquite thorns, and my feet from brambles below, Burton and I continued on down to the bridge to join the others. When we got there, Alex was sitting alone in the middle of the bridge.

The wind kicked up, making things even more miserable, but if anyone else noticed, they didn't say anything. Alex began to chant in a language I assumed to be from the Tonkawa. The three of us watched in silence until I could stand it no longer. "John," I whispered, "do you know what he's chanting?"

"Not sure, but I think he's talking to my mother."

No sooner than those words escaped his mouth, she came.

She did not materialize completely, but appeared as a faint ball of light that floated just in front of Alex. Alex continued to chant, getting louder and louder. The ball of light seemed to get excited and bounced from side to side.

Suddenly, Alex got down on all fours, howled, and disappeared. Poof! Just like that—nothing left. The ball of light disappeared also. This was going to make even the Wolf Dance seem like child's play.

"John, what just happened?" Burton asked excitedly as I gasped aloud.

"I'm not sure, but he is with Mother. He will not come back tonight, so let's go home."

"Just like that—go home?" we chorused.

"Yes. They will return together when they come. Together, they have strong medicine and Big Elk will help guide them. They also have the shaman's ear. They will be safe."

Chapter Eight

FINALLY, NANCY LEFT FOR HER weekly shopping trip with her sister. They were so predictable. Nancy and her equally fat sister always spent Thursdays in Tonkawa shopping, trading-- whatever it was that they did. He didn't care as long as she brought back the tobacco he wanted and craved. She used to bring him alcohol as well, but the local moonshine was stronger—and cheaper.

Lately, Nancy had questioned Black Tooth as to why he spent so much time over at Big Elk's place. It wasn't like Big Elk left anything of value behind. Everyone knew Big Elk was destitute. He'd spent all his energy and money rescuing poor or sick tribal members and stray cats. He was an idiot. He could've gotten rich off of them, but no, he wouldn't take any money for his charity. Maybe then Black Tooth would've inherited something besides a run-down shanty house and an out-dated Cadillac.

Big Elk never married, and for no better reason than the fact that Nancy kept him well-fed, he deeded everything to Black Tooth in his will. Big Elk never trusted his cousin, but he was very fond of Nancy and wanted to repay her kindness to him. If he'd known Black Tooth would betray him unto death, he would've put a curse on him earlier. Ah, well, never too late...........

Black Tooth opened yet another box only to find more dried

herbs, feathers, and some tiny little teeth that had once belonged to a deceased mammal of some type or another. Tossing that aside, he dragged another dozen shoeboxes out of the closet. Surely it was here someplace. He was certain the tribal rumors were true that Big Elk had gained possession of the highly-coveted ear belonging to El Mocho. When he found it, he would use its powers to get rich. His tribe would then give honor to him instead of that charlatan in Texas. He'd show Nancy who was boss then. She'd plead for him to take her to his bed instead of sneering at him behind his back.

***

"Maw-maw, are you not tired and in need of rest?" inquired Alex. He and Minnie had spent the night scouting the land around the Yegua. Alex was concerned about his aging grandmother. Although he saw her only in wolf form, she was gaunt, had a crippling gait, and exhaustion filled her eyes. He saw something else too—a fierce determination like he'd never witnessed from her before.

"Yes, my boy, I am tired, but time is running short. We must find El Mocho's cure together. With your help and strength, we will find his grave, wherein lies the secret to heal our people."

"But, how will we know where that place is?"

"We will know when we reach it, my boy, keep your eyes and ears open, for mine are weak."

The pouch hanging from around Alex's furry neck quivered slightly. "Keep searching—do not quit now."

In response, Alex let out a long, blood-curdling howl which brought terror to his own human heart. This existence was strange to him and he wasn't sure of the return path. If anything happened to Minnie, he was trapped.

***

It had been two whole days since Alex had disappeared with Minnie out on the bridge. I was a nervous wreck wondering where they were and what it was they were searching for on my land.

Burton tried to suppress his anxiety over the situation, but even he was showing signs of distress.

Our wedding was only two weeks away and we both wanted this situation resolved before then.

"Mother!" yelled Sandra. I flinched and dropped a soapy dish on the kitchen floor. Pieces of my butter bell skied across little pools of water and came to a stop.

"What's got you so jumpy, Mom?" she inquired as she helped me clean up the mess.

"Nothing, just didn't hear you coming."

"Ever the nervous bride, right?"

Covering up the real reason for my anxiety, I simply agreed.

"Did you and Kassie have a good day today, Mom?"

"Yes, we did, as a matter-of-fact. She's in the den watching TV, why don't you ask her for yourself?"

"I think I will."

"Hey, Kas, did you and Nana have fun today, kiddo?"

"Yep, we watered Nana's flowers and went for a walk."

"Where'd you go?"

I listened from the kitchen to see what Kassie would tell her mother. Earlier in the day when we walked down by the creek, Cooter went off into another of his rages. Certain he must be hearing (or seeing) Minnie and Alex, I pretty much ignored him and tried to keep Kassie entertained.

All along the creek I had seen two sets of wolf tracks which did not go unheeded to my granddaughter's young eyes. She pointed them out to me and said, "Cooter sees the wolves, Nana, and there they go now, into the trees."

Why she could see them this time and I could not is beyond me, but at least I knew they were both alive and well. Maybe Burton or John had figured out a way to help Minnie and Alex by now. They were supposed to meet for lunch and discuss the situation.

***

Later in the evening, Burton slowly made his way home. He looked tired, so I offered to make him a sandwich and some hot chocolate. I was anxious to know what he and John Williams had discussed during their lunch meeting, but remained silent until he was ready to talk.

Finally, mid-sandwich, Burton summarized their meeting. They both knew something needed to be done soon as Minnie was tiring and Alex needed to get back to his classes at A&M. Therefore, the two of them were going to spend the next day walking my pasture and the creek bottom in search of any clues previously missed. They figured that two heads were better than one.

The game plan was to use the cabin as home-base and Burton asked if I would mind being the chief cook and bottle washer. "Not really," was my response, "but don't you think that three of us might cover more territory than two could?"

He couldn't argue that point, so I was included in the search party the following morning when John arrived.

We had an impromptu meeting around my kitchen table to

discuss a plan of action. "Let's begin with what we do know," advised Burton.

"We know that Minnie and Alex are looking for something— presumably a cure for diabetes. We know that Big Elk had diabetes, and we know that he gave El Mocho's ear to Minnie. So, I would assume that Alex and Minnie are searching for some sort of prescription left behind by a previous shaman when the tribe lived here on the Yegua and that this "ear" is going to somehow help them."

"Yes," said John, "but we also have the dung beetle left as a clue and I can't see where that fits in."

"Neither can I, but we'll keep that information on the back burner for now. We all have our cell phones, so call if you find anything interesting. Otherwise, we'll meet back here at the house at 11:00 for a break."

***

The three of us started off together, but soon split up into our assigned sections of the pasture. We had decided to walk the pasture first, later concentrating on the creek bottom. Burton took the western-most section nearer the Yegua, I took the middle, and John had the eastern third to prowl.

I wasn't too sure what I was looking for, but enjoyed the fresh air anyway. I had on my boots and my weathered khaki hat. It was a beautiful fall morning, making it easy to forget that two lives were hanging on today's search.

My eyes were glued to the ground as I walked down, down toward the bridge. Nothing out of the ordinary was to be seen. A flurry of white-wing doves startled my reverie, reminding me why I was here, so I continued my descent slowly to the ravine. It was a chore to remain vigilant, but step by step, I surveyed my surroundings for clues of our missing friends—or anything out of the ordinary.

As my undisciplined mind continued to wander, I realized that the land was getting dry once again and we needed rain. Little dust clouds rose around my boots with each step taken. Looking up to my right, I spied John bending down to look at something. Must not have been important, for he soon rose and kept walking, head bent to the ground.

To my left, Burton's long legs had taken him much further than John and I had gone, but he seemed completely engrossed in his mission. Before long, we had all reached the back fence and took a water break. So far, none of us had seen anything worth sharing.

My heart went out to John as I felt his sense of urgency to find Alex and Minnie. I could only imagine how I would feel under the same circumstances—however far-fetched. Dark circles under his eyes betrayed the fact he'd had little to no sleep the past couple of nights. Matted hair fell from under his ball cap as he removed it to scratch an itchy spot, and contrary to popular belief, this Indian had quite some beard stubble going for him.

After a short rest, we split up again, each taking a different path back to the cabin. Determined to be more vigilant, I started up the west side where Burton had walked before. John was now in the field's center, with Burton on the eastern side near the county road.

Guiltily, I heard my stomach rumble and began to think about what I would fix for lunch. Geez, couldn't I concentrate for even five minutes? Head back down, eyes on the ground, keep walking.........

A couple of times I noticed Burton or John stop to examine the ground, but each time, they rose to continue walking toward the cabin. It was starting to get rather warm, so I removed my jacket and got a drink from my water bottle. Since the sun was almost overhead, I assumed it was near or past 11:00. After a quick check on my cell phone, I saw it was 11:05. I was about to call Burton and suggest we break for lunch when I heard John.

"Here, here—I think this is it!"

Burton and I immediately began running to the spot where John stood. As we approached, we saw what John saw. There in front of him, not far from the tank dam, was a small rise in the land. On top of that stood a medium-sized mesquite tree, branches low to the ground. The sky had clouded over, leaving a single sunbeam to shine down on that tree like a spotlight. And, there, beneath the tree was a dung beetle rolling a ball of cow droppings for all its worth. Lastly, as if to say, "I told you so," was a broken deer horn akin to the elk horn in Minnie's pouch.

The three of us hugged and rejoiced together for a good five minutes before we could think what to do next. Finally, we gave in to hunger pangs and headed to the cabin. Our plan was to eat, rest, and return with shovels to see what lay hidden beneath that mesquite tree.

***

An hour and a half later, three excited adventurers walked back to the site with shovels in hand. Burton and John had rigged up a wire screen to filter the dirt as we dug it out to make sure we didn't miss anything of importance.

We laughed and giggled like school children on a field trip. There was still some nagging anxiety, though, as to Minnie and Alex's safety since we'd seen no traces of them all day.

John was the first one to arrive back at the tree even though he carried the heaviest load—the wire screened box. "You've got to be kidding!"

When Burton and I arrived, we saw what had disturbed our friend. The exact spot where the dung beetle was found had already been excavated down about three feet. The hole was about three feet in diameter as well. "What on earth?" I questioned.

Upon closer examination, John pointed out claw marks in and around the hole. "Alex! It must be Alex. Mother is too weak to do anything like this."

With that, John threw himself into digging the hole even deeper while Burton and I sifted the dirt that came out. Within a half hour, we'd found two arrowheads, some empty snail shells and an old, rusty horseshoe. Not used to such physical exertion, John soon tired and he and Burton exchanged places.

Another half hour, more trash and a few rocks later, we still had not found anything of interest, save the arrowheads and horseshoe. We all sat down to take a much-needed breather. "This has to be the spot. I know Alex was here—I can feel him. I just wish I knew exactly what we were searching for though," lamented John.

Cooter had followed us back to the tree after lunch and had been chasing butterflies, grasshoppers, rabbits, or anything else that moved, for most of the afternoon. Mostly, he had ignored us, but now that we'd sat down, he inched in for some attention.

Out of habit, I pitched him a chewy treat which, for once, he ignored. "Humph," I thought to myself, "someone's getting spoiled."

Before we knew it, Cooter was down in that hole digging with all his little mutt strength. Dirt came flying out on all sides. Cooter was having the time of his life and howling to beat the band!

"What is it, boy? Whatcha got, Cooter?" asked Burton as we all charged the hole.

There, at the bottom of the hole, under that shaggy little pooch sat an urn made from ancient pottery. John motioned for Burton to remove it, which he did most carefully after lifting Cooter up to me. Dirt fell from its dark sides as Burton raised it up to John. Strange markings covered the outside and the top opening was covered in layers of dried bee's wax.

Soon, John and I sat in awe as Burton gingerly took his pocketknife and removed the bee's wax plug. "Normally, this would be done under stricter conditions, but under the circumstances, we'll forgo the formalities," informed the professional archaeologist.

Tiny piece by piece, the wax relented and turned loose of the urn. Excited, but afraid of the contents, I held my breath as the final bit was removed. We sat in silence as Burton slowly turned the urn upside down and gently shook out its contents.

A small leather scroll came sliding out into Burton's hands. Brittle, but still in tact, it revealed strange markings resembling hieroglyphs I'd seen in magazines.

Not knowing what to do next, we simply carried the urn and its contents back to the cabin.

Chapter Nine

ALEX HAD SEEN THE HUMANS gathered on the other side of the pasture. Who were they and why were they interfering with his mission? His mind was playing tricks on him in this new existence—it was getting hard to remember who or what he had once been. His ancestors called to him from every direction, and it was confusing. The pouch around his neck was a curse—it allowed him to hear too many things, but he could no more remove it than stand upright on two legs.

He'd had to leave his elderly companion behind as she could no longer keep up with him. But, without her guidance, it was hard to stay focused on his quest. In desperation, Alex decided to return to the place where he'd last heard El Mocho calling to him. When he arrived, he saw what the people had seen earlier—the dung beetle, the horn, the sunbeam. What was it they meant? Alex knew they were significant, but why?

The voice was weak, but it told him to dig! For ten, twenty, thirty minutes, Alex's strong forepaws threw dirt out of the hole and scattered it in all directions. The voice grew louder, encouraging him to go deeper, but he heard other voices too—vaguely familiar voices that were scrambled in his brain. The humans were coming back!

He wasn't sure if they could see him, or if he should fear them, but he hurriedly escaped to find his companion— to make sure she was still alive. When he found her, she was alert with her eyes focused on the people. Together they watched as the man pulled El Mocho's urn from its earthly home.

Alex searched the grizzled face of his small companion for answers. "What does this mean?" he questioned.

"The man has found it--- work here is done. Time for us to return... before too weak," the companion gasped.

***

Within the hour, Minnie and Alex lay quietly under a pin oak tree not far from the cabin. Both were exhausted from the transformation back to human form. While clearing his mind, Alex gazed at the old woman beside him wondering who she was. Her breathing was labored and it took every ounce of strength for her to open her wizened eyes. Something about her was familiar—mostly her gnarled hands. He'd seen those hands before, and drew comfort from knowing that about her.

Alex slowly stood on uncertain legs and surveyed his surroundings. What was this place? How did he get here and exactly who was this poor little woman? As his memory and his strength returned, Alex realized that it was his beloved grandmother lying on the ground. He must get help for her. Gently, he stroked his grandmother's head and told her, "Maw-maw, just rest. I am going for help and will return soon. Just rest, okay?"

Minnie reached up, took his youthful hand in hers and brushed her cracked lips against it in a kiss—a gesture he'd never been privy to before. Hesitant to leave, but knowing it would be quicker than trying to carry Minnie, Alex raced across the field on two legs instead of the four to which he'd become accustomed.

The cabin Alex had seen from the field looked familiar to him now and he remembered that he had come with his father to the

Johnston place to help find his grandmother. Little by little, his memory and strength returned, and he ran faster knowing that his grandmother's fragile life rested on his shoulders.

Reaching the cabin, Alex burst in unannounced. The little group at the kitchen table was aghast at his sudden and disheveled appearance.

"Alex!" cried John. "Are you alright, Son?"

"Yes, Father, but Grandmother is in bad shape. I had to leave her back at the edge of the woods. She needs to get to a hospital as soon as possible!"

The three men jumped in Burton's diesel and lit off across the pasture in short measure. I called the hospital to inform them we'd be bringing in an elderly woman who'd been lost and exposed to the elements for a number of days.

By the time the men returned with Minnie, I had backed my car out of the driveway in order to follow them to the hospital. I silently prayed God would take care of Minnie and let her live to help her people another day.

***

Nancy and her sister, Little Dove, made it home just before dark. Nancy dropped Little Dove off at her house and began driving up the winding road to the house she shared with Black Tooth. She was concerned about her husband. He was loosing weight, anxious all the time, and could not sleep. Sometimes he would scream out in the night as if he were being scalped, but when asked, would tell her it was nothing. His moodiness bothered her as well. He often yelled at her for no reason and ordered her to stay away from Big Elk's old house.

Nancy knew Black Tooth was down at Old Charley's drinking moonshine because she'd seen his shiny, new Chevy pickup there.

She'd seen it sticking out from behind the shrubs in Charley's backyard earlier when she took her sister home. Good! That would give her time to do a little prowling in Big Elk's house. Maybe she'd discover what it was Black Tooth didn't want her to see.

Nancy turned off the car lights and walked up to the front door of Big Elk's ramshackle shotgun house. She'd been there many times over the years, but had only been in the front room and the kitchen, which were the first two rooms of the elongated home. Since Big Elk was single, Nancy thought it not proper to visit long when she came, but had always seen to it that the old man was taken care of.

Even after Minnie Williams, Big Elk's elderly cousin from Texas, came, Nancy still took food over to the sick man. Singing Bird was Minnie's Tonkawa name, but Nancy did not think it fit her well. True enough, Minnie was as skinny as a bird, but her voice grated on Nancy's last nerve every time she spoke. And, she doubted the woman could sing a single note.

Nancy could also tell that Minnie didn't care for her either. The last time Nancy had seen Big Elk alive she had mistakenly interrupted some sort of meditation or séance the two were holding. As she had always done, Nancy had burst into the kitchen with a pot of chili and banged it down on the stove. Big Elk was too weak to give much response, but Minnie all but threw her out on her ear. The nerve of that woman!

But, tonight Nancy had her opportunity--there was no one to keep her from snooping—and snoop she would!

***

The ER staff was ready and waiting for us when we arrived with Minnie. They were on the curb with a gurney as Burton's pickup screeched up to the sidewalk. With no trouble at all, Minnie's emaciated body was whisked onto the rolling bed and taken away.

John and Alex accompanied the gurney as Burton and I parked

our vehicles. Together, we walked silently into the hospital. Not long after we entered, I realized that this was my first time to be back in an ER waiting room since Heb's accident. Funny how certain places and smells can awaken our memories like that.

All the old feelings washed over me anew and tears began running down my cheeks. Trying to mask my emotions, I quietly pulled out a Kleenex from my purse and dabbed my moist eyes.

Thinking I was concerned about Minnie, Burton held my hand and gently squeezed. I didn't tell him the real reason for the tears.......

About an hour later, John and Alex came into the waiting room to give us an update on Minnie. They informed us that Minnie was dehydrated and malnourished (which we already knew). Also, the doctor had ordered a few more tests to be run because of her irregular heartbeat.

If nothing suspicious showed up, she possibly could be placed in a room some time later in the night. The intravenous fluids were beginning to give her a little strength and she had spoken weakly, albeit, incoherently just before an oxygen mask was put over her mouth and nose.

We all knew Minnie would fight to the death to finish the task set before her by Big Elk. The question in all of our minds was whether or not Alex could take up the mantle should Minnie not survive.

***

Nancy's search of Big Elk's house had not turned up anything out of the ordinary. Everyone knew he was a healer and kept lots of herbs, potions and plants around. He was also a hoarder, so there were stacks of junk everywhere. "How do people live like this?" she thought to herself.

Thinking she'd return and look again later, she decided to finish examining Big Elk's desk and head on home. She'd already been through all the side drawers, so she concentrated on the big, long drawer in the center. It had a ragged crack near the key hole, so she'd have to be careful or it'd fall apart.

Nancy was so focused on her task that she failed to hear the pickup coming up the dirt road. Black Tooth had worn out his welcome and been sent home early by Charley's new woman who didn't appreciate his vulgar, drunken mouth. She sure was uppity. He didn't understand why Charley would put up with a woman like that. It wasn't like she was purty or nothin'.

"What the hell? Who'd be up there in Big Elk's ole shack?" Black Tooth turned off the truck's headlights and drove up the familiar dirt road in the dusky light. Instinctively, his hand landed on the butt of the old rifle which he always carried to kill snakes, coyotes or other annoying critters.

Nancy's car soon came into focus as Black Tooth rounded the last bend in the road and rolled to a stop. "That bitch! I'll teach her a lesson she won't forget. Teach her to disobey me........"

It's hard for a drunken man to tiptoe, so Nancy heard Black Tooth long before he reached the second room of the little shack. Knowing she couldn't outrun him, she quickly slipped Big Elk's little brown book into her purse and braced herself for the attack.

She quietly peeked around the door and panic struck fear in her heart. Black Tooth had hit her before, but the drunk fool was carrying a rifle! While her eyes searched for the door she knew was somewhere in the back room, Nancy picked up one of Big Elk's raggedy slippers and threw it behind her staggering husband.

As hoped, he turned and obliterated the shoe and a good square yard of the floor surrounding it. Nancy took advantage of the distraction and made it to her car just a few seconds before he focused in on her.

With a "ping- ping," and finally a "whiz" before she slammed her car door, Nancy quickly turned the ignition key and peeled out of the driveway.

Driving as fast as she dared on the rutted-out old road, Nancy steeled her nerves. She knew Black Tooth would try to follow her, and a good head-start would certainly keep her healthy longer. Good thing she'd filled the car with gas earlier in the day because she wasn't going to stop for a long, long time.

Soon she was off the reservation and heading to a friend's house in Oklahoma City.

***

Minnie was prepped and ready for surgery early the next morning. Although it was clear that she wanted to communicate with Alex, it didn't happen. Her heart was definitely out of rhythm and a pacemaker was going to be inserted.

Burton and I had returned to the hospital to support the family throughout the ordeal. By the time we arrived, Minnie was already in the operating room.

"Mornin', John, Alex," began Burton.

"Thank you for coming. I'd like you to meet my wife, Hope. Hope, these are my friends, Joan and Burton. As you know, they helped with the search for Mother."

"Hope," we chorused.

While the men visited, I sat with Hope who was a strikingly beautiful woman with rich brown hair tied loosely in a ponytail. She was younger than I had imagined—hardly old enough to be Alex's mother, but it was easy to see where he got his good looks.

Hope informed me that their two daughters were in school. They wanted to shield them from the knowledge of the severity of the situation if at all possible. The oldest, Lily, was a freshman in high school, and Jaycee was in fifth grade. Even though it had been clear that Minnie favored Alex, the girls adored their grandmother. It would hurt them terribly for her to pass away.

The five of us sat huddled together for some time in silence, each left to his/her own thoughts. Sooner than expected, the surgeon entered the room. From the fear in our eyes, it was clear to him what we were collectively thinking.

"No, no, she's fine!" he exclaimed. I just came to tell you that we'll be putting her in a room as soon as she comes out from under the anesthesia. Why don't you all go get a bite to eat and you can see her when you get back?"

***

About an hour after leaving Big Elk's house, Nancy was 100% sure that Black Tooth had not followed her. The fool probably thought she'd come home in a day or two like she'd always done before. Feeling safe now, she pulled her sedan off the freeway and stopped at a convenience store to relieve herself and get something to drink and eat. Next, she would call her friend and make sure she had a bed for the night.

Squeezing back behind the wheel, Nancy searched her purse for her cell phone and saw Big Elk's brown book. In her panic to escape, she'd forgotten all about it. She turned on the overhead light and turned to the first page—just some notes about a cure for warts. The next page was similar and had drawings of some strange plants. On and on she quickly flipped through the pages.

About half-way through the book, she noticed that Big Elk's handwriting had taken on a sudden shakiness. It became more difficult to read, but one thing was clear. He thought someone was poisoning him!

Oh my goodness! Surely he didn't suspect her! She would never do anything like that—he was like a father to her. Frantically, she read on and hit a brick wall when the last few pages were in a language she'd never seen before.

Chapter Ten

AFTER A SHORT VISIT WITH his grandmother, Alex's parents insisted he return to A&M so that he wouldn't get further behind in his studies. He promised her he would return the following weekend to receive further training regarding El Mocho's instructions.

Arthritic fingers clung to his arm in a last attempt to keep him with her, but he reluctantly said, "Maw-maw, you need your rest now. Dad and Dr. Mosley have El Mocho's urn and will work on deciphering its message. You've done your part for now. Whatever has been in that grave for the past couple of hundred years can wait another week. Just get well.......and, Maw-maw, I love you."

With that, he walked out the door and Minnie was resigned to the fact that there was nothing else she could do—for now.

***

With Minnie safely in the hospital, and Alex in College Station, I anticipated that my life would return to normal. Burton was back at work and I had the day to myself.

Cooter and I had just come in from a leisurely walk along the Yegua and were headed for the house when my cell phone rang. I didn't recognize the number, but took the call anyway thinking it could be related to Minnie. She hadn't rallied as quickly as we had all hoped, and I was a little concerned.

A woman's unsteady voice came over the line, "Who... who have I reached?"

Not feeling threatened by this timid woman, I answered, "Joan Johnston. Who are you trying to find?"

"I'm not sure. Can you please tell me where you are?"

"I'm in Texas near a little town called Lexington. Who is this and where are you?"

"Oh, good," she replied with an obvious sigh exuding from her throat. She seemed too upset to respond to my questions.

"Do you need help?" I inquired.

"Yes, I am looking for Minnie Williams. I think I have some important information for her. Do you know her?"

Feeling the need to protect Minnie, I said, "Why do you ask?"

"My name is Nancy. I met Minnie recently when she was up here in Fort Oakland, visiting our cousin, Big Elk. Big Elk passed away recently and I found this little journal he had been writing in. Minnie's phone number is written inside the cover, but she's not answering her phone. Below her number, are some other numbers, but no names. You were the first one to answer.

Not elaborating on the details, I simply told Nancy that Minnie was in a hospital near here and that she was not doing too well. I offered to give her John's phone number explaining that he was Minnie's son.

"Thank you, Joan. This is extremely important. I need to talk to someone before my husband finds me. I appreciate your help." That said, the line went dead.

I immediately wrote down the phone number shown on my phone and called Burton. He was on his lunch break and took the call.

"Hello, Sunshine, what's on your mind?" he cheerfully answered.

"Burton, I've just had a call from Big Elk's cousin's wife in Oklahoma. She was looking for Minnie and said she had some important information for her. I told her Minnie was in the hospital and gave her John's phone number. Burton, I think this woman is in danger. She was hiding from her own husband of all people. Said she had some little book that had belonged to Big Elk."

"Hmmm......that is interesting. That little book may hold some very important information. I'll check with John later on this evening to see if he's heard from her. What did you say her name was?"

"Nancy is all she said, and from her conversation, I gathered that she was still in Oklahoma somewhere-- and very frightened."

"Okay. Guess all we can do for now is wait. Want me to pick up something for supper or you feel like cooking?"

***

Black Tooth returned to Big Elk's house the next morning after he'd found Nancy snooping around. Showed her, he did. That wench would listen to him the next time for sure. By the way, where had she gone? He'd been too drunk to follow her very far, but she always came home after their arguments.

Oh well, he could manage on his own a few more days without her. She'd come crawling back like she always did. But, then again, this is the first time he'd actually shot a gun at her. Perhaps?? Nah...... she'd return.

With this still on his mind, Black Tooth entered Big Elk's rickety, old house. The screen door almost fell off in his hand as he pulled it open. Glancing around the dilapidated room, he spied the shoe he'd shot full of holes the night before and it frightened him. He hadn't remembered firing off so many rounds. He knew he'd shot at Nancy a few times trying to run her off, but now he feared he had actually hit her!

What if she went to the hospital or to the tribal police? There would be an investigation. No, he couldn't afford an investigation. He had to find Nancy first.

***

John's phone rang just as he left the parking lot at work. He quickly pulled his BMW into the closest lane of traffic and answered. "Hello?" he mindlessly said while checking his rearview mirror.

"Is this Minnie Williams' son?" the unfamiliar voice asked.

"Yes, is she alright?" he hesitatingly wanted to know.

"I don't know. I haven't seen her in awhile. This is Nancy, Big Elk's cousin's wife up in Oklahoma. I reached a lady named Joan Johnston earlier and she gave me your number. I understand your mother is in the hospital?"

"Yes, yes, I thought this was the hospital calling me. You say you're Big Elk's cousin's wife? You are Black Tooth's wife?"

"Not for much longer I'm afraid," the frightened woman replied. "He tried to kill me a couple of nights ago because I was going through some things in Big Elk's house. He'd warned me to stay away, but something kept telling me I needed to go have a look for myself."

"He tried to kill you over that?"

"Yes, and I think I know why now. I need to come see your mother as soon as possible. I believe I have something that Big

Elk intended for her to have. He passed away very suddenly before he could give it to her. Would it be possible for me to drive down there—maybe tomorrow?"

***

Alex tried to concentrate on the lecture, but his mind kept returning to the events from the past weekend. Had it been a dream? Had he really been trapped in a wolf's body for a couple of days? That was just too crazy to believe, but it did happen. What would his friends think if he told them?

He looked down at his hands, nails cut, cuticles clean. How different they'd looked just a few days before. He remembered seeing long, thick claws caked in dirt digging up the ground over El Mocho's grave—thought about using those same claws to scratch at fleas that congregated behind his hairy ears.

Well……better listen to the professor for now. He had a lot of catching up to do so he could return to his grandmother. She had some unfinished business for him, and he needed to be free for the weekend.

***

John called Burton later that evening while he and Joan dined on Elgin sausage, potato salad and beans Burton had picked up on his way home. Wiping barbeque sauce from his lips, Burton flipped open his phone and answered.

"Burton, this is John. I've gotten a rather interesting call from a woman from our tribe in Oklahoma. She says she's married to Black Tooth who is a cousin to Big Elk. Says he tried to kill her a few nights ago when he found her going through Big Elk's things. He'd forbidden her to enter Big Elk's house but she went anyway. Long story short, she found a little book that she thinks Mother should see and is heading this way tomorrow. I'm going to meet her at the hospital after work. Would you like to come along?"

"By all means. About 5:30 you think?"

"Perfect. See you there."

Burton picked up another sausage link and started cutting into it with his knife and fork before he realized I was staring at him.

"Well?" I impatiently asked.

"Well, what? Not much to add to what you already know. This Nancy woman called John like you expected and is driving to the hospital tomorrow to give Minnie the book she found at Big Elk's house. I'm meeting them there after work. End of story."

"I'm coming with you," I blatantly said.

"No, you're not," I received in return.

When I looked up in shock, I saw a fierceness in Burton's eyes that had never been there before, but I challenged anyway, "And just why not?"

"Because I don't want you involved until I know what's really going on. This situation could get really nasty before it is all over. The less you know, the safer you'll be, and that's that."

Knowing he was right didn't make me any happier, but I conceded and began cleaning up the dishes in silence. I finally came to peace with the realization that my involvement could inadvertently lead to some ill-will coming to my own family. The thought of something happening to Sandra, Jack, or the girls was unbearable—so, for once, I would back off and mind my own business.

***

Back in Fort Oakland, Black Tooth tried Nancy's cell phone, but she wasn't answering. That worried him even more. Where could she be? He really hadn't paid much attention the night she left—just chased her long enough to scare her.

He called her sister's house expecting Little Dove to answer, but Tall Joe answered instead. Black Tooth hated his brother-in-law, but chose to be polite in order to gain some much-needed information about his missing wife.

"Hey, Joe, is Little Dove home? I need to ask her a question."

"Yeah, just a minute, I'll get her."

Checking his irritated mood, Black Tooth waited for Little Dove to come to the phone. "Finally," he thought when she answered. He knew he had to play this right or Little Dove would slam the phone down in his ear and not tell him anything.

Using the sweetest voice he could muster up, he asked just enough questions to figure out that Little Dove had no idea where her sister could be or even that she was gone. He knew she told the truth because she had this annoying way of snorting when she didn't want to tell you something or fibbed to you.

So, Nancy hadn't gone to her sister. He didn't think any bullets actually hit her either. There wasn't any blood in Big Elk's driveway, so he chose to believe she was just hiding—but where?

She must have seen or found something in Big Elk's house, or else she would've called him by now and cussed him out for shooting at her. They would've had a huge fight and he'd beg her to come home. It was always that way with them—always had been. Sometimes he'd have to spend a night in jail to sleep off the alcohol, but eventually they'd make up.

"They will find out soon."

Spinning around, Black Tooth searched the room and found no one. "Damned hangover," he said aloud-- mostly to still his own nerves. But deep inside, he knew this was not the result of a hangover. His body began to shiver, then shake violently.

***

Nancy knew she had made the right decision to drive to Texas when her friend, Linda, answered the phone. It had been Black Tooth looking for her. Linda played it off well, but Nancy was more frightened than ever. Knowing that she was not the one who poisoned Big Elk, she had deduced that it had been her husband. Had he not had the opportunity every time he took her food over to his cousin's house?

Without the statement in Big Elk's book, no one would've suspected he'd been poisoned. He'd been sick for some time with diabetes so no one was surprised that he died, just surprised he'd gone as fast as he did.

She was sure that Big Elk intended for Minnie Williams to have the book because of the secret writings in the back. They didn't make any sense to Nancy, but she was fairly certain Minnie would understand them—at least in part. Not that there was any love lost between her and Minnie, but she did love Big Elk and wanted to avenge his murder. Besides, she needed to put some distance between her and Black Tooth. He would never suspect she was hiding amongst his own family in Texas.

Soon, he would regret shooting at her, and he would regret being the mean, drunken murderer that he was. He would never belittle her or hit her again because soon he would be incarcerated on death row. That thought alone gave her the courage to proceed with her plan.

Chapter Eleven

BURTON WAS IN HIS OFFICE trying to decipher the message found inside of El Mocho's urn. He knew that the Tonkawa had no formal written language, so the symbols El Mocho used must've been known only by the medicine men or women in his tribe. After a couple of hours, Burton was no closer to the answer than when he started. Perhaps the only thing he could do would be to take the parchment to Minnie at the hospital. Possibly she would understand its meaning if she was physically and mentally up to the challenge.

After taking several photos of the outstretched parchment, Burton rolled it up and placed it into his briefcase. He had one staff meeting, two grad-student conferences, and one class to teach before he could leave for the day. He was excited about the hospital visit which would include John, Minnie, and Nancy.

Before he left his office, Burton made one final call. "Hello, Joan, just reminding you I won't be home for supper tonight. John and I will most likely take Nancy out to eat in order to get more information from her. From what John tells me, Nancy and Minnie didn't quite hit it off in Oklahoma and she might talk more freely away from the hospital."

"I didn't forget, Hon, I ran into Sandra before she left for work this morning and she invited me over to eat with her and the girls.

Jack's working late tonight on some 4-H projects at school. He said he'd eat in town, so this worked out well for all of us."

"You're not still upset that I don't want you at the hospital visit?"

"No, I understand, but I do want details when you get here!"

"Done! And.......Joan?"

"What?"

"I love you." And before I could reply, the line went dead.

***

John arrived at the Taylor Hospital early thinking he would sit in the parking lot and watch for Nancy to arrive. He was half afraid she'd back out at the last minute and he didn't want that to happen. With the windows down and the radio on, his fingers kept beat with the soft rock tune coming through the Beemer's radio.

Ten minutes passed and his growling stomach reminded him he'd skipped lunch again. It was getting to be a habit—working through his lunch break. Well, that was okay because business was good. It needed to be good with Alex in school and two more to put through college in a few more years.He didn't mind working hard if it meant Hope could be a stay-at-home mom. She did that so well—mothering, that is. His children were well-cared for to say the least. He was totally in love with her, and for some reason unknown to him, she was crazy about him too.

When Hope looked at him, she didn't see the scars that marred his once-handsome face and hands. After weeks in the hospital, she continued to nurse him at home. Seemed she just loved him more after that.

Remembering that fateful night brought a surge of sadness over

John. He would never forget the screams of his father as he struggled to free himself from the wrecked vehicle. They'd just left the feed store in Elgin with a truck bed full of chicken feed, dog food, and some onion plants Minnie'd asked for when a drunk driver plowed into the passenger side where his father sat.

John had hit his head on the steering wheel knocking him unconscious for a moment. When he came to, the truck was on fire. He undid his seatbelt and struggled to release his father whose leg was pinned under the seat. Multiple times he tried to help dislodge the helpless old man, to no avail.

Thinking he would try from the outside, he'd jumped out of the driver's seat. It was then that bystanders pulled him away. Before he could fight them off, there was a huge explosion and it was all over. The nightmares still plagued him......

Immersed in his thoughts, John pulled a package of sunflower seeds out of the glove compartment and opened it. He hurriedly ate a handful and downed it with water from the bottle he habitually kept in the console. Then, he impatiently searched the parking lot for signs of Nancy or Burton.

Burton drove up in his old Volkswagon. Since John had never seen Burton in the VW, he was expecting the pickup. Undetected, Burton parked a row behind John. Quietly, he opened the door, uncoiled his long legs and grabbed his briefcase. Knowing how jumpy John could be, he took advantage of the situation and sneaked up behind him.

"Hey, John. Looks like you're in your own little world in there!"

"Dang, Mosley, you've got to quit scaring the crap out of me!"

"I thought Indians didn't get scared."

"Well, this one does, so cut it out, man!" But, he smiled as he firmly shook his friend's hand.

Burton took the liberty of opening the passenger door and climbing in before continuing, "Any sign of Nancy?"

"No, she told me she was driving a white Honda Civic though. Thought I'd watch for her and escort her up to Mother's room. Don't want her chickening out on us."

"Yeah, I can understand her hesitation alright. If someone had taken a few pot shots at me, I'd be a little leery too." Another minute went by before Burton spotted her, "Think that's our girl right there, John."

The two men got out of John's car and headed in Nancy's direction. She had already seen the two men and assumed they were the ones she was to meet. She took a final look at herself in the mirror and grimaced. Not much she could do about her appearance now. It took every ounce of courage she could garner to open the car door and get out, but she knew this had to be done—for more reasons than one.

As the men approached, Nancy took off her sunshades, revealing dark circles beneath fearful eyes. Her hair was neat, but her clothing crumpled from the long drive to Texas. It was apparent that Black Tooth's wife was under a great deal of stress.

"Nancy?" John asked.

"Yes," she meekly replied. Normally she wouldn't be so demure, but being off the reservation, tired and fearful, she couldn't help it.

"Nancy, I'm John, and this is Dr. Burton Mosley. He's been working with Mother for a couple of years now and is a trusted friend. He's also an archaeology professor at the University of Texas and quite qualified to assist us in completing the task Big Elk entrusted to my mother."

Nancy's eyes searched the pavement beneath her feet as she uttered, "Good to meet you."

"Please, just call me Burton, if you don't mind."

"Okay," was the only word Nancy could muster.

"Good, well, let's go, shall we?"

Together, the trio entered the hospital and quietly entered the hallway where Minnie slept in Room #224. Burton had kept a firm grip on Nancy's arm just in case she decided to bolt. John peeped in and was again reminded how frail his mother was. She was still on oxygen and the only nourishment she'd had for days was liquid. Her tiny chest heaved up and down laboriously.

"John, is everything okay?"

"Yes, Burton, she's sleeping that's all."

Minnie's still-sharp hearing picked up on her son's voice. Her husky voice managed to whisper, "John?"

"Yes, Mother. I'm here with Dr. Mosley and we have brought someone else to see you."

With that, Minnie lifted her tired eyelids and focused on the little group which had just entered her room. As recognition finally settled in, Minnie pointed a bony finger in Nancy's direction and screeched, "Out!"

"No, Mother, Nancy's come to help. She has brought you something from Big Elk's house."

Gaining courage, Nancy stepped forward and spoke to Minnie, "I don't blame you for being upset. I know you thought I was eavesdropping on you and Big Elk, but all I wanted to do was bring him food."

"Food! Your food made him sick!"

"I know that now, but let me show you what I have."

Nancy gingerly fingered Big Elk's leather book and drew it out of her purse. She hesitatingly gave it to John and pointed to the scrawled handwriting. He read aloud, "Someone is poisoning me and I think I know who it is."

At this, Minnie's eyes fiercely glowered at Nancy, and she spit in her direction. She began chanting quietly and rocking side-to-side. Burton had to admire the old woman's spirit, but was secretly glad he was on her good side.

"It wasn't me. I loved Big Elk—he was like a father to me. When he started getting ill, I always made sure he had something to eat. But, it was Black Tooth who usually took the food over to Big Elk, and I think he's the one who put poison in it. I don't know why he would do that though. Big Elk was old and frail and everyone knew he was going to die soon anyway."

John handed the book to Burton who, in turn, offered it to Minnie. A thin, sinewy arm came out from under the covers and took the little book. Her hand shook violently as she stared at the page.

Tired, cloudy eyes strained to see the trembling print. Minutes passed as she struggled to turn the tiny pages one at a time. The little group surrounding Minnie's bed watched with anticipation. Finally, Minnie let out a little gasp and let the book drop down on the sheet.

"Black Tooth is guilty," Minnie stated without emotion, or apology. She pulled the little book under the covers and closed her eyes.

It was clear to see Nancy's relief, but now she knew she could not return to the reservation until Black Tooth was in custody. Her life was worth nothing to him any more.

Her strength exhausted, Minnie soon fell asleep, a light snore filling the room. John silently reached under the blanket, took Big Elk's book and put it in his pocket. His mother would be very angry with him for doing so, but he couldn't risk loosing this critical piece of evidence against Black Tooth.

Burton knew the parchment would have to wait until another time. It was enough for now to have to deal with Nancy and the murder investigation John would initiate. Minnie was too exhausted for anything else at the moment.

The three visitors left without saying goodbye and walked down to the main lobby. Nancy excused herself to the ladies' room and John asked Burton to wait for her so he could phone the tribal office in Oklahoma.

***

"John Williams here, Nioka. I need to speak to the Chief, is he in?"

"Yes, John, is everything alright?"

"If you mean with Mother, she's resting in the hospital. She's very frail and still isn't eating, but we hope to see some improvement soon."

"I hope so. We heard she had been missing and that your son found her.

After loosing Big Elk, we certainly don't want to loose Minnie as well. Too many of our elders are gone from us already. Here's the Chief."

"Chief, this is John Williams. I'm afraid I have some disturbing news to report...."

***

"Joan, I've just left the restaurant with John and Nancy. I hope I'm not in hot water, but I'm bringing you a house guest."

After a brief, but blood-chilling explanation, I readily agreed to have Nancy come to the cabin. John and Burton had decided she

105

would be safer with me rather than with a family member. Until Black Tooth was apprehended, her life was in jeopardy.

An hour later, Burton pulled into the driveway followed by Nancy's Honda. He directed her to pull her car around back by the barn and helped her with her meager belongings.

I opened the back door and watched them walk up to the house. Burton had to shorten his stride to accommodate Nancy's short legs. From Nancy's frazzled appearance, it was obvious she needed some rest. My heart went out to her. I could not imagine having my husband shoot at me and then find out he'd been slowly murdering his own cousin!

My arms embraced this timid, fragile woman as I welcomed her into my home. After making her comfortable in the extra bedroom, I returned to the kitchen to visit with Burton.

He caught me up on all the details, and together we decided he would stay out in the camper as long as Nancy was with us. We felt she would be more at ease with that arrangement, and he wanted to be close by just in case there was trouble.

***

Meanwhile, in Oklahoma, an investigation was begun to find out whether or not Big Elk's death was premature. Quietly, in the middle of the night to avoid suspicion, Big Elk's body was exhumed and taken to the state medical examiner. Only two tribal members were in on the excavation, and they were sworn to secrecy by the Chief.

Ironically, they had to drive past Black Tooth's house to get to the cemetery. It was hard to believe he had it in him to poison his own cousin. Black Tooth was lazy, deceptive, and hard to get along with, but −murder? Then, there was Nancy. Most everyone in the tribe wondered why on earth she stayed with Black Tooth so long when it was well-known how badly he treated her. Surely she'd leave him after being shot at, even if the autopsy cleared him of murder.

The soil around Big Elk's grave was still loose and damp from recent rains, so digging him up wasn't as bad as they expected. Soon the hole was refilled and the corpse placed in the back of the pickup. Ever so quietly, with headlights turned off, the truck made its way back down the hill and past Black Tooth's house.

"You will be found out, Black Tooth," muttered a soft, eerie voice in the dark of the bedroom.

Black Tooth immediately sat up in bed and looked around the room in fright. Cold sweat broke out on his forehead and he shook uncontrollably. "Idiot!" he said to himself. "Big Elk is dead—you're dreaming." He attributed the shakes to his worsening diabetes and tried desperately to get back to sleep.

***

The next morning, Nancy, Burton and I ate a late breakfast and discussed our plans for the day. Since Burton needed to work at the office, he kissed me goodbye and walked out the door. Nancy seemed rested, so I inquired, "Nancy, would you like to drive into Austin and pick up a few things? I have a rather extensive grocery list and I thought that maybe there were a few things you could use as well."

With adverted eyes, she shyly replied, "No, thank you. I will just stay here if that is okay?"

Silently kicking myself, I realized that Nancy had no money. Certainly she'd left the reservation in haste to escape Black Tooth's vengeance, and even if she had a credit card or checkbook, he could trace them to her and possibly find her location if she used them.

"Nancy, what if I loaned you some money? You'll need some extra clothes and toiletries while you're here. It won't be a problem, I assure you."

"I can't take your money, Miss Joan."

"You won't be taking it-- you can pay me back any time, or if it'd make you feel better, you can help me out around here instead of paying me in cash."

Her eyes lit up at this thought. "I am a good cook, Miss Joan. I will do my best to earn my way."

"Good, it's a deal, but it's plain Joan, not Miss Joan,okay?"

"Now, would you like to go with me to Austin? It'll be fun and we'll try out a new restaurant I heard about from a friend."

Chapter Twelve

ALEX TRIED HIS BEST TO study for his upcoming chemistry exam, but his mind wondered restlessly. He'd called his mother for an update on Minnie, but she was rather evasive in her answer. This bothered him as he felt his mother was protecting him from the truth as she always had. But, he wasn't a child needing protection any longer— and he needed to see for himself that his grandmother was okay.

El Mocho's ear rested in the bottom of the closet in Alex's dorm room. He'd carefully put it inside a small box and hidden it with some of his belongings. Brian, his roommate, seemed like a nice guy, but was overly enthusiastic about prying into Alex's business at times. He wanted to make doubly sure Brian didn't snoop around needlessly and stumble onto the ear.

Since his return to human form, the ear had not revealed any more secrets for Alex, so he felt that maybe he should take it to his grandmother and seek her advice. One thing was for sure—he wanted to get rid of the heinous body part as soon as he could. The hours spent in another creature's body had left him emotionally confused and the voices from the past haunted him.

Alex made up his mind to drive to Taylor and see his grandmother as soon as his last class ended the next day. He would take the ear with him and decide what to do with it then.

***

Nancy and I returned home after a wonderful day of shopping in Austin. It was fun to help her pick out a small wardrobe consisting of everyday wear, plus a nice dress for my wedding. She was reluctant about attending, but I assured her she would fit right in with the rest of our friends and family.

Taking Nancy to the mall was like giving candy to a child. Her eyes eagerly took in all the Christmas trappings and gaudy shop windows. It seemed too early for Christmas, but for once, I was glad to see Santa before Thanksgiving.

We found our way into a large department store and located the ladies' apparel. I quickly found a few items I wanted to take on my honeymoon while Nancy shopped a few aisles further over.

Eventually, she picked out a stylish brown dress accented with turquoise trim and went into the dressing room. When I found her, Nancy was standing in front of a three-way mirror admiring the way it hugged her ample form. Thick, wavy hair hung around her face, and it was obvious she had once been a very beautiful woman. She twirled round and round in complete and innocent oblivion.

I felt like an intruder and wished I could make myself invisible, but it was pure delight watching her enjoy herself so. Suddenly, she looked up, saw my reflection in the mirror, and her countenance fell. "You must think I'm silly," she said abashedly.

"Not at all, Nancy. I think you're beautiful. I'm just afraid you'll outshine the bride in that gorgeous outfit! All the men will be staring at you!" I teased. "Now, let's find some shoes that match and go eat."

***

Burton pulled his truck up beside the travel trailer and got out. He was greeted by Cooter, Emma and Kassie. He scratched Cooter behind the ears, picked up a giggling girl in each arm, and marched through my kitchen door.

"Look what I found in the backyard!" he grinned. Each girl wiggled and squirmed to be released, but he only held on tighter. Finally, his arms gave out and he gently set them down on the floor.

Suddenly, they calmed enough to see that I had company and stared at Nancy, who now wore a bright red polyester warm-up suit and tennis shoes. Her hair, however, had been braided into two long plaits with her turquoise earrings dangling beside them. It was obvious to Emma and Kassie that Nancy was not from around here.

"Girls, I'd like you to meet my friend, Nancy. She's here from Oklahoma and will be staying with me for awhile."

"Hi," they shyly chorused while hiding behind Burton's legs.

Nancy, meet my granddaughters. The tall little blonde is Emma and the short curly-haired one is Kassie.

"Hello, girls. How old are you?"

Burton pushed them forward to answer, but they still clung to his pant legs. Seldom were my granddaughters that shy, but they'd never seen an Indian before.

"Emma is six now and Kassie is almost four," I answered for them. "I think the cat's got their tongues."

"Are you a real Indian?" Emma asked shyly—her hazel eyes aglow.

"Yes, I am, Emma."

Gaining courage, Emma continued, "Do you live in a teepee?"

"No, our people haven't lived in tepees for a long time. I live in a house just like you do."

Kassie, who was too young to understand much about Native Indians, simply crawled up into Nancy's lap and lovingly stroked her long braids. "Pretty," was all she said.

"Girls, does your mother know you're over here?" I asked.

Burton interrupted to say, "Not unless she saw me kidnap them from the backyard!"

"Why don't we all go over there and we can introduce Nancy to your mom and dad?" I suggested to the girls.

"And Cooter, too," Kassie chimed in.

"Yes, and to Cooter, too," I responded with a smile.

***

Later that night at the hospital, Minnie had decided she was going home. It was of no concern to her that she hadn't been dismissed by her doctor. She silently pulled out the IV in her arm, took off her oxygen nose clip and got out of bed. Her shaky legs threatened to give way beneath her, but she was determined to leave.

Quietly, she peeked down the hall at the nurse's station. There was only one nurse on duty and she was occupied with the computer screen at her desk. Minnie closed the door to her room and sat down on the cold tile floor.

She began softly chanting and rocking back and forth—back and forth. Surely she had enough energy left to do this one last time. She could not stay in this hospital one more day. They did their best to help her, but she needed her own medicine, and she needed to go home and finish the quest Big Elk sent her to do.

Thirty minutes later, the night nurse began the rounds of her patients. When she came to Room 224, she saw that the door was tightly shut. Funny-- it had not been closed earlier and she hadn't seen anyone enter the room. She knocked softly and went inside only to find it empty. After a brief search of the ground floor, the hospital went into lock-down mode and all the floors were checked and rechecked. Minnie was not to be found anywhere.

***

Hope was awaken from a sound sleep by the ringing of the phone beside her bed. "Yes?" A pause, and then....... "Are you sure?"

"John, John, it's the hospital. Your mother is missing! They've called the police, but no one saw her leave her room and no one entered. They've even checked the hospital's cameras to be sure."

"Give me the phone," he demanded. "At what time did you notice she was gone?"

After a brief conversation, John said to Hope, "I'm going down to Mother's house. Stay here."

***

Earlier in the week, Black Tooth had tried to trace Nancy's phone, to no avail. Where had that woman gone and what did she see or know? Her disappearance was making him really nervous. People were starting to ask questions. Thus far, he'd been able to put them off, but Nancy's sister was getting to be a real pain in the ass. She called every day wanting to talk to Nancy, but he always made up some excuse. Little Dove wasn't having any more of that and was on her way over to his house.

He decided that this was a good time to go deer hunting, not that he enjoyed deer hunting. Black Tooth quickly threw a few things into his truck, grabbed his rifle and shells and headed out the back door.

He threw the truck into gear and peeled out as quickly as he could. No point in being a sitting duck when Little Dove got there. That woman was a menace and a force to deal with. He had no intention of letting her interrogate him one on one.

In his haste, Black Tooth drove a little too fast past the tribal offices, squealing his tires. Nioka took notice as she sat at her desk opening the morning's mail. Thinking it unusual for Black Tooth to get in a hurry about anything, she also realized she hadn't seen Nancy in a few days. Nancy generally stopped by to chat after picking up her own mail at the post office. Oh well, maybe she was out of town visiting friends or something.

Soon, Black Tooth's truck was headed north toward Stag Creek. He was going to an old deer camp he'd often visited with his father when he was a boy. He hadn't been there in years and was hoping the old cabin remained. No matter. If it had fallen in, he'd just sleep in the truck for a couple of nights and then go home. Surely Nancy would have returned by then.

After a good twenty minutes, Black Tooth turned off the pavement and onto a dirt road.It looked as if no one had driven it in some time. Weeds had overgrown the ruts, making them difficult to follow. He thought this was the right path, but he didn't trust his memory 100%.On and on he went, searching intently for some familiar landmark to guide him. There, on the left! There was the tall cottonwood tree where he'd shot his first deer. He remembered sitting under its canopy waiting for his father to come show him how to bleed out the little buck.

Those were good days—days before his father died and left him behind to be raised by a drunken grandfather who beat him. His mother had died giving birth to him, so he never knew what it was like to have her love. Maybe it was a good thing he and Nancy never had any children. He wouldn't have been a good father. Like his grandfather, he loved the bottle too much.

Black Tooth steered the truck past the old cottonwood and around the bend towards the creek. The road only worsened, having been eroded by timeless rivulets of water seeking lower ground. Undeterred, he pushed forward. Finally, the deserted old cabin came into view.

Stopping near the front door, Black Tooth turned off the engine and stepped down from the truck. The outside of the cabin had some wear, but remained intact. Vines wrapped their tendrils in and around the log walls, giving them an eerie appearance. He had to push aside some brush to reach the front door, but, to his surprise, it swung open with ease.

Black Tooth gingerly stepped inside and looked around. The sparse little room was dirty and full of cobwebs. There were signs of mice around, and the roof had a few holes in it, but for the most part, it was solid. "Yes, this will do nicely," he thought to himself. Within the hour he'd lit a fire in the old fireplace, plugged the holes with some old rags he'd found, and made himself comfortable.

***

John put on his clothes and hastened down the hill to his mother's house. He felt certain that whatever had befallen his mother had been of her own volition. She'd seemed so frail when he last visited her that he could not imagine her walking out of the hospital by herself. But then again, she'd surprised him before.

Since it was only a stone's throw from his own house, John's strong legs took him quickly to her little shack. If she was there, she hadn't turned on any lights. As he stepped up onto the back porch, he noticed the guineas nesting in the rafters. Dodging their droppings, he made a mental note to get rid of them, or at least move them into the old chicken coop.

He pushed open the sagging door and turned on the kitchen light. Room by room he searched the little house for signs of his mother. It seemed nothing had been touched, nothing out of place or missing. Fear gripped his heart as he thought of all the possibilities.

Despair and exhaustion overtook him as he dropped down into Minnie's worn-out rocking chair and cried himself to sleep.

About an hour later, his chilled body awoke to a strange sound coming from outside. John instinctively grasped the knife in his pocket, ready to defend himself if need be. Silently, he opened the knife and stood up. If someone had come to steal, he'd be greatly surprised to find an armed Indian waiting on the other side of the door.

Sharp ears and eyes remembered their early training as John assumed the position of a young brave on the attack. He crouched behind the door waiting for it to open—but nothing happened. Deciding to go on the offensive, John crept to the window nearest the door. As he did, the ancient wooden floor creaked in defiance, making him wince.

Slowly, stealthily, John peeked around the window frame and scanned the front yard from left to right. He saw no one. Thinking he'd better search the sides and back of the house also, he moved toward the kitchen and the back door. No sooner than he'd taken the first step, he heard it again-- a low moaning sound—one he could not identify.

John decided the best plan of action would be to go out the back door and circle around to the front. Whoever, or whatever, was out there seemed unaware of his presence and would not be expecting him. Hoping the guineas would not give him away, he quietly slipped out into the darkness.

Quietly, he cursed his mother's obsession with plant collecting. There must've been a hundred or more tin cans, old pots and jars to dodge on his way to the front of the house. He'd be lucky not to trip and give his position away. The shadows darkened the further he went, making it almost impossible to see where his feet took him.

Finally, he rounded the side of the old shanty and peered into the moonlight shining on the front porch. Barely visible in the dim light lay a grayish-white body. There was no movement, no sound emitting from the creature's long snout.

Chapter Thirteen

ALEX QUICKLY RAN BACK TO his dorm and threw a few things in a duffle bag for the trip to the hospital and then home to Elgin for the weekend. In his haste, he almost forgot the mummified ear hidden in the bottom of his closet. He hastily locked his car, ran back up the stairs, and to his dismay, ran smack dab into his roommate, Brian.

Brian was taken by surprise and jumped aside as Alex blew threw the door. He had a strange look on his face and his hand was on the closet door—Alex's closet door. Quickly, Alex assessed the situation as Brian blurted out, "Dude, you scared me! Your closet door was open and some of your things missing. I thought someone had gotten into our room."

Breathing a sigh of relief, Alex answered, "No, man. I told you my grandmother was in the hospital, remember? I need to go see her, that's all. Finished my last class with Dr. Lohrmann at 2:00, so I'm outa here."

"Is she worse?"

"I don't know, just have this feeling, you know? Forgot a couple of things and came back for them."

With that, he picked up a textbook (which he really didn't need), grabbed the box in the bottom of his closet and hurried down the stairs. He pulled out of the dorm parking lot, winding his way over to University Avenue. Within ten minutes, he was on Highway 21 heading west to see Singing Bird.

A little before 5 p.m., Alex pulled up to the hospital and took the elevator to his grandmother's old room. He was stopped in the hallway by an attendant who told him that his grandmother was no longer there. He was given no further explanation, so assumed she'd gone home. He got back into his car and drove to Elgin.

***

The same morning Black Tooth had gone deer hunting to avoid her, Little Dove drove up the hill to his house to confront him. She didn't trust Black Tooth any further than she could throw him and knew he was not telling her the truth.

It was unlike her sister to ignore her phone calls. She'd left several messages on her cell phone, and all had gone unheeded. She would get to the bottom of this one way or another.

As she rounded the last bend in the dirt road, she noticed that Nancy's Honda was gone as well as Black Tooth's shiny, new pickup. No matter.......she'd go inside and look around. That sorry brother-in-law of hers better have some good explanations on hand, that was for certain.

Little Dove slammed the car door and stormed up the uneven walkway. As she reached the front door, she couldn't help but notice that most of the plants on the porch were dead or dying. Unlike Nancy to let her plants go to waste like that. Some of those pots contained herbs they'd shared over the years—herbs Nancy used in her daily cooking. Now she was more suspicious than ever.

She yanked on the stubborn screen door and then shoved the wooden door until it bumped up against the doorstop and came to a quivering halt. Immediately, her sensitive nose picked up an unpleasant odor. Alarm rising in her throat, she followed the nasty scent into the kitchen. Dirty pots and pans sat all over the stove and the trash hadn't been emptied in days. It was obvious her sister had not been there for some time.

After searching each room of the house, Little Dove noticed that Nancy's toothbrush, makeup and other toiletries had been left on the vanity in the bathroom. Her sister would never have left those behind if she planned to be gone one night, much less for days.

Ten minutes later, Little Dove marched into the tribal offices in the village. "Nioka, I need to speak to Red Hawk, is he in?" she questioned her old friend.

"Certainly, Little Dove, should I tell him why you're here?"

"Damn right you should. Nancy is missing and I think her sorry-ass husband has something to do with it!"

"Black Tooth?"

"Of course, Black Tooth, who else?"

"He flew past here in that new truck of his about an hour ago. Never saw Black Tooth get in a hurry before."

"Mm-hmm—he got in a hurry right after I called the SOB on the phone! He didn't want to talk to me and got outta town. Just like him. Where's the Chief?"

***

True to her word, Nancy took over my kitchen the morning after our shopping trip. Having never had a maid in my life, it was a luxury to have someone else cook for me. A titillating aroma permeated the house, teasing my nose awake. After a slow stretch, I got out of bed and ambled into the kitchen to see what was taking place.

When I got there, all I could see was Nancy's ample rear end as she bent over to pull a tray of steaming hot cinnamon rolls from the oven. I thought I'd died and gone to Heaven. "Never trust a skinny cook," was the adage that ran across my mind, and "Mmmm-mm," was all I could say.

Nancy turned around with a toothy smile that would melt butter. "I hope you like them. I used to make them for Big Elk all the time—Black Tooth too, but he didn't appreciate them the way Big Elk did."

"Oh, honey, you can make them for me any time, and believe me, I will appreciate them!"

Before I could pour myself a cup of coffee, Burton walked in the back door. "I'm not sure what smells so good, but count me in! Mornin, Sunshine-- Nancy."

Nancy demurely nodded, and I him a peck on the cheek. With a twinkle in his eye, he reached over and gave Nancy a bear hug. Not knowing what to do, she froze in place and stared at me.

"Nancy, you'll have to learn to just swat that man out of your way or he'll bug you to death!"

With that, he turned on me and plastered a big, wet kiss on my lips.

"Behave yourself, you're outnumbered, you know," I lamely threatened.

By this time, Nancy had placed a platter full of rolls on the table and poured another cup of coffee for Burton. For a large woman, she was quick on her feet in the kitchen. It was also easy to see I wasn't going to be the only one she would spoil.

We finally convinced Nancy to sit down and eat with us, although she was still shy and reserved. She mostly listened to our conversation and blinked those beautiful doe eyes over the top of her coffee mug.

Her thick, ebony braids hugged her breast, and I wondered how long it took her to get them so congruent, so perfect. I self-consciously ran a hand through my own unruly locks and thought of my up-coming appointment at the beauty shop.

When she finally did speak, we both were taken aback. "Excuse me, I don't mean to interfere, but it seems to me that you two haven't had much time together since I've been here. Why don't you go spend the day together somewhere? It would be good for you and I don't mind staying here by myself. I was often alone at my house on the reservation so I'm used to it. Go—have a good day and I'll fix you a wonderful meal when you return."

Burton and I looked at each other as if to say, "Why not?" and gratefully thanked her. We both headed for a shower and agreed to meet in 30 minutes on the patio.

***

John knelt down beside the limp creature on the porch and desperately searched for signs of life. There were none. Her nostrils were still damp and warm, so he knew it hadn't been long. "If only I'd found her sooner," he lamented. He tenderly closed her eyelids and lay down on the hard plank porch beside her. Placing his head on her chest, he pulled his legs up into a fetal position and stroked her shaggy pelt. He felt like crying again, but he was too empty inside.

When Hope found him, he was still there, shivering head to toe. Frost clung to his hair and clothing. She called his name, but he said nothing. Finally, he let her take his hand and help him to his feet. Silently, together, they carried Minnie into the house and lay her on her own bed.

***

After Little Dove's visit with Chief Red Hawk, there was an APB put out for the arrest of Black Tooth. The coroner's report had

121

also come back and there were traces of rat poison found in Big Elk's body. The Chief sent a couple of his deputies out to search both men's houses and declared them crime scenes.

Bad news always traveled quickly throughout the reservation, and there was great speculation as to Black Tooth's whereabouts and what he'd done to send Nancy into hiding. He'd had plenty of time to leave the state as well, but there were no leads to go along with that theory either.

Most of the villagers had known Black Tooth all of their lives and not a few would be happy to see him behind bars. Although he aspired to be their spiritual leader/healer, there were few who would've trusted him with either their spirits or their health. He mostly was known for his dishonesty and deception—as well as for his excessive drinking and meanness. It was hard to believe he was related to Big Elk who had been highly esteemed among the tribal members.

***

Burton and I drove up to his house in Austin and packed some more of his things to bring out to the cabin. It was hard to believe that we would actually be married in ten days. I elected to clean the kitchen since I didn't have a clue what he'd want to pack for the cabin.

The boxes were piling up in the hallway and I wondered where on earth we'd put them. I figured we'd be building another room or two onto my little cabin soon if the packing went on much longer.

The barn had a rather sturdy loft which could be used for storage, but the mice always took a toll on anything out there. So........it was either add on or be cramped for space. Oh well, we'd cross that bridge in a few weeks. The wedding was upon us and we both were excited about that and the honeymoon cruise to follow.

As I scrubbed the kitchen sink, I overheard Burton talking to someone on his phone. His voice grew louder as he walked toward the kitchen. Whoever was on the line must have had bad news as my fiancé's rugged face was tight and grim.

"I'm really sorry, man. Let me know if there's anything we can do."

Burton sighed heavily as he looked up and simply stated, "Minnie's dead."

"Oh, Burton. That's awful. That family has been through so much lately, and now this."

"I know. She made it home last night but died on her own front porch. John found her around midnight. They're having the body taken to her family in Oklahoma for an Indian burial. The Justice of the Peace ruled heart failure, but we all know it was more than just that. She pushed her frail little body way beyond its limits."

***

A single phone call came in saying a fire had been spotted in the northwest corner of the reservation near the headwaters of Stag Creek. As was her custom, Nioka had taken the office's emergency phone home with her, so she immediately set off the alarm calling all able-bodied men to action. Eight tribesmen of various ages and sizes soon climbed aboard the old fire truck and set off in the direction of the creek.

The contrast of flame and forest was accentuated by the light of a full moon. The men on the truck were hoping they would be able to contain the fire quickly so they could return home to their warm beds. Often that was not the case, though, and they would have to call in for reinforcements.

Later that same night, Nioka's phone rang again. "Nioka, send the Chief up here. We're up at Signal Hill near Stag Creek. There's something here he needs to see. Tell him to hurry."

When Chief Red Hawk arrived in his Jeep, the fire had been 75% contained. Buffalo Dog had waited at the highest bend in the road to escort him to the site of the old deer hunter's cabin. When they arrived, they saw the chimney still standing and lots of smoldering logs. A fire truck sat nearby being emptied onto the remaining wall. Remarkably, Black Tooth's new Chevy pickup sat unharmed about 25 yards away. As they got out of Buffalo Dog's vehicle, the scent of burning flesh overcame them, sending them back to the confines of the truck.

The two men had seen a lot in their day, but this would remain in their memories forever. No one liked Black Tooth, but to die like this.........? They would close off the area and complete the investigation in the morning. There wasn't much more they could do for Black Tooth tonight anyway, assuming it was Black Tooth.

***

Burton and I got home around 6 p.m. The back of his truck was loaded down with boxes, so he parked near the barn to unload them. I reminded him about the mice, but he assured me he would go through his things and take out anything that he prized and bring it to the house.

I walked on up to the cabin while he finished unloading the truck and saw Nancy through the kitchen windows. She was stirring something on the stove and I was anxious to see what we were having for supper.

"Hey, Nancy! What's for supper? It smells heavenly."

"Indian stew and cornbread," was all I could get out of her as she busily set the table. "Go wash up and get Mr. Burton," she instructed. "My cornbread is hot and ready to eat."

Not quite knowing how to take this new, bossy Nancy, I simply suppressed a grin and obeyed. It was good to see her regain some confidence and pride in herself.

Before I had time to go ring the dinner bell on the back porch, Burton brought himself through the kitchen door. "Nancy, I don't know what you got cookin', girl, but I can't wait to sink my teeth into it!" he exclaimed.

I couldn't help but notice that he got a big smile instead of orders to wash up like I did. The man was a charmer, that was for certain.

Nancy directed us to our seats and served us as if we were the King and Queen of England. She refused to sit down and eat with us, saying she'd sampled enough while she was cooking.

After we each put away two bowls of delicious stew, Nancy opened the refrigerator and pulled out dessert—homemade tapioca pudding. I was beginning to think that Nancy didn't ever need to go back to Oklahoma.....

Finally, Burton wiped his face with his napkin and asked Nancy to sit down.

"Nancy," he began. "First of all, I want to tell you what a wonderful meal that was. You are one fantastic cook. But, I have some bad news to tell you."

Nancy's smile faded, and her eyes filled with apprehension.

"Minnie Williams has passed away. John found her late last night at her house. She'd somehow managed to get herself home in spite of her frailty."

"Oh, no," was all Nancy could get out at first. Then she continued, "We didn't understand each other, but she was a good woman and was trying to help our people the best way she knew. Big Elk thought highly of her too. I am sorry for John and his family."

After an uncomfortable silence, I changed the subject. "Nancy, Burton and I would like to ask you to house-sit for us while we're on our honeymoon. You wouldn't be totally alone since the kids are next door and my neighbors, the Kaufmans, will be home. What do you think?"

"I would love to do that for you!" she quickly replied. "I still don't know where Black Tooth is and I fear for my life. If he was mean enough to poison a kind, old man like Big Elk, he wouldn't think twice about hurting me."

"Good. Then it's a deal," smiled Burton.

Chapter Fourteen

The Williamses accompanied Minnie's body to Oklahoma in order to give her the proper funeral and burial befitting a member of their native tribe.Since he had been chosen to follow her path in healing, Alex would have an important part in the ceremony. He didn't feel important. Like a lingering, misty fog, depression choked the very breath out of him.

Alex's sisters loved Singing Bird also, but were not as close to her as Alex had been. Being the eldest grandchild, only grandson, and the one chosen to inherit Minnie's powers as a tribal shaman, Alex had formed a special bond with his grandmother. Even as a young lad, he could be found helping her re-pot herbs or trailing behind her in the woods hunting for special plants or mushrooms. He had an uncanny knowledge of nature from an early age on. While his kindergarten contemporaries learned their colors and alphabet, Alex learned about the phases of the moon, alkaline and acid soils, and the uses of green moss verses that of lichens.

Now, more than ever, he determined to make his grandmother proud of him. Yes, he would accept the mantle as shaman of his tribe. He would return to Oklahoma some day, but first he would get his degree in medicine and become a full-fledged medical doctor. That was the best way he could help his people-- his grandmother's people.

***

Nioka handed the phone to Chief Red Hawk and said, "Chief, the phone's ringing now."

Chief Red Hawk quickly picked up the receiver in his office and waited for someone to answer.

I was washing up a few dishes as Nancy put the finishing touches on our lunch. It was just the two of us since Burton had driven into Austin to teach a couple of classes.

"Hello," I absentmindedly answered while watching a bushy-tailed squirrel munch sunflower seeds stolen from the bird feeder.

"I'm looking for Nancy Runningbear, Black Tooth's wife. I understand she is staying there?"

"Who is this?" I defiantly asked.

"Chief Red Hawk from the Tonkawa Tribal Office in Fort Oakland, Oklahoma," was his reply.

"What makes you think she is here?" I innocently asked.

"John Williams came by here earlier today with his mother's body so we could begin her funeral preparations. He gave me this number. I assume you know John?"

"Yes, yes," I replied in a more humble tone. "Nancy is here. Just a minute."

With fear in her eyes, Nancy hesitatingly took the receiver. I noticed the tremble in her hand as she put it to her ear. "This....... this is Nancy."

"Are you sure?" she insisted and waited for the reply. After listening solemnly, she said, "Thank you for calling," and dropped the phone.

Fearing her legs would give out beneath her, I quickly grabbed her elbow and led her to the kitchen table. I poured a cup of leftover coffee and set it in front of her. "Nancy, what's going on?"

"Black Tooth is gone," she sobbed hysterically.

"Gone as in run away, or gone as in deceased?" I inquired.

"Dead! He was found burned to death in a fire up in an old hunting cabin on the reservation. Drank himself into a stupor and couldn't get out after the fire started. My sister thought I was dead, too, until John Williams arrived and told them I was alive."

I stood up, held Nancy in my arms and rocked her like a baby. She sobbed for what seemed an eternity, and when I released her, the front of my tee shirt was soaked. Finally, she stopped crying and pushed me away. "I am sorry, Joan, I've ruined your shirt."

"Silly, it's just wet, not ruined," was my simple reply.

After a short period of silence, I asked her, "Nancy, what do you want to do? Will there be some sort of funeral that you'll want to attend?"

"No, no funeral. Black Tooth was a murderer and our tribe will not honor him in any way. After today, I will not mourn Black Tooth either. He is gone and out of my life forever. If it is okay, I'd like to drive home tomorrow and then come back for your wedding next week. I can still house sit while you and Burton are on your honeymoon."

"Of course, Nancy. Now that you're safe, you do whatever you feel is best for you. Don't feel obligated to come house sit, though. Sandra's right next door and she can keep an eye on things for me."

"You don't understand, Joan. I want to house sit for you. That will give me some time to decide what I want to do. I've inherited Big Elk's house as well as all of Black Tooth's property. There's no way I want to live in either house, but I do have some important decisions to make."

***

That evening, I met Burton down by the Yegua as planned. He had gone down earlier to build a fire beside its cool, churning water while I packed a picnic basket with cheese, crackers, fruit and wine. Nancy, in her grief, had retired early and we didn't want to disturb her.

Burton looked up as I neared the fire and smiled wickedly, "Hey, Baby. Watcha got in that basket?"

"Oh, just a little snack for my boyfriend," I teased back with a fake Marilyn Monroe voice.

His face softened as he called my name, "Joan?"

"Yes?"

"I'm happy. Just wanted you to know that."

"Me, too," I replied nonchalantly and gazed into my beloved's eyes for reassurance. Firelight reflected off his dark eyes like little meteor showers as I leaned into his kiss.

We sat down on the old blanket I'd tossed on the ground and unpacked the basket. Silently, an almost- full moon rose on the horizon while the evening stars tip-toed across the universe. We sipped our wine slowly and allowed the gentle beauty of the evening saturate us.

Meanwhile, across the Yegua, a congenial owl softly asked, "Whooo? Whooo?" In reply, a lone coyote began its high-pitched wail, bringing a chill up my spine. I leaned into Burton and he wrapped his long, protective arms around my body.

We sat in silence for a long time, letting the autumn night work its magic. The Yegua's rhythmic solo gurgled along while Mother Nature played the background music. We became drunk on more than the wine, but I guess true love is more like yeast. Once it's mixed into the dough, it's invisible, but the results undeniable. Our relationship was sort of like that yeast— growing, maturing....

Tired and a bit tipsy, we were lost in the moment and failed to notice the four-legged creature approaching our blanket. Stealthily, quietly, it stalked its prey. Inch by inch, it crept upon us, unconcerned for its own safety. Neither of us was aware of any danger until its hairy fur brushed up against my elbow and warm saliva ran down my arm.

Simultaneously, I screamed and rolled away from Burton. Gravity then took over, pulling me down toward the murky water and into the oozing mud. My sweetheart looked over at me with a gleam in his eye and laughed, "Cooter, your timing is priceless!"

***

Early the next morning, Nancy left for northern Oklahoma. Now that she no longer feared for her life, she called her sister, Little Dove, to tell her where she'd been and reassure her that she was safe. Little Dove insisted she stay with her when she got to the reservation and Nancy had readily agreed. Her fear of Black Tooth was gone, but had been replaced by a powerful superstition. There was no way she was spending the night in her old house.

All afternoon, Little Dove watched the driveway for signs of her sister's car. In preparation for her visit, she cleaned out the extra bedroom and baked Nancy's favorite dessert—pear pie. Her skinny, little husband had complained a bit about Nancy staying with them indefinitely, but one look from Little Dove put a stop to that nonsense. He knew not to push her too far or she'd cut him off-- not only from their bedroom, but from her cooking as well! The bedroom he didn't mind so much, but her tasty cooking he'd miss.

Nancy's car made its way through the reservation just as the sun was setting over the large cottonwood at the top of Eagle Mountain. Eagle Mountain was really just a hill, but got its more glorious name from one of the late chiefs who had a spiritual encounter there with an eagle.

She drove slowly now, thinking about the friends or family behind each door. It saddened her to know that her husband had been such an evil influence among these people. Although it was no fault of her own, it embarrassed her to have been married to him. For years, she worked tirelessly to undo the bad things he did. If she knew of something he'd stolen, she'd return it quietly to the owner. Sometimes he'd beat her if he found out. Finally, she'd just given up and left him to his own devices. She always had a feeling his life would end tragically—as it had.

As she passed the Tribal Offices, Nancy saw Black Tooth's truck parked in the rear. That truck was almost brand-new. Last year, Black Tooth decided he wanted and deserved a new truck, all-the-while, insisting Nancy's old, second-hand Honda was good enough for her. Remembering that conversation renewed some of the repressed hostility she'd often felt towards him. She hadn't been allowed to drive his truck, and had only ridden in it once. Well, now it was all hers—if she wanted it.

Within minutes, Nancy was at her sister's house. She opened the car door, stretched her tired legs, and walked up the narrow sidewalk. Little Dove met her on the door stoop and squeezed the breath out of her like she'd done when they were kids. "Let go!" Nancy finally gasped. "I'm fine."

"I know you're fine now, but for several days I thought you were dead, so let me hug you!"

Arm in arm, the sisters entered the house. Tall Joe didn't bother to get up, but did grunt a greeting as Nancy entered the room. She wasn't too fond of her brother-in-law, but took a moment to pat his shoulder as she passed by his chair.

After putting Nancy's things in the spare bedroom, the two women sat down at Little Dove's kitchen table to talk over coffee and pie.

"Nancy, have you had time to think about what you'll do long-term? You know you're welcome here as long as you want to stay."

"The only thing I'm sure about is that I will sell my house as well as Big Elk's. I don't want to live in either one of them. But, right now, I don't know where I do want to live. Tomorrow, I'd like for you to go with me to pick up some of my things. I don't want to be alone in that place. Later, I'll go to Big Elk's and see if there is anything there of value."

***

Back at the Yegua, Sandra and I sat in the gazebo and drank a glass of tea. It was a lazy Sunday afternoon—warmer than usual. My daughter's long, blonde hair glistened in the sunlight, contrasting with her warm, almond eyes. My thoughts turned to Heb and the day we brought her home from the hospital. He didn't want to put her down—insisted she needed to be rocked for hours on end. Maybe that's why they were so close; it was that early bonding.

Our family was beginning its second year without Heb and I'd be lying if I said I didn't still miss him. We all did.

"Penny for your thoughts," Sandra inquired with a smile.

"Oh, I was just thinking how all of our lives have changed over the past year, that's all. Guess I was just missing your daddy a little too. Must be the holiday season that's made me a bit moody."

"I know what you mean, Mom, I miss him all the time. There's some days I wake up thinking I need to tell him something, then I remember he's gone."

Before we could get too melancholy, Jack, the girls, and Cooter all ran up the slope from the pasture. The girls were giggling and out of breath. Cooter, who didn't quite get the game, barked excitedly anyway. Apparently, the girls had challenged their dad to a race, making him run backwards as a handicap. Much to their delight, Jack tripped over a gopher mound and fell to the ground. Both girls piled on top of him and tried to pin him down. He wrapped his long legs around them until they begged to be released. No sooner than he let them go, they began a leaf fight......

It didn't take long for them all to give in and join us in the gazebo. We poured a few more glasses of tea and relaxed in the warm Indian summer air.

Finally, Jack announced he was taking the four-wheeler out to the far pasture to check on a heifer that was about to calve.

"Daddy, Daddy, take us too," the girls begged with fake pouts.

My son-in-law was a sucker for his two little imps and soon gave in. "Okay, but you have to stay in the four-wheeler and you have to be quiet. Can you do that for me?"

Without answering, their feet hit the ground running for the barn.

"Wait for me!" was all Jack had time to say.

Sandra and I finalized our Thanksgiving plans for the family, who would then return the next day for the wedding. She had taken over Thanksgiving to allow me time to finish shopping and pack for my honeymoon cruise. She planned to keep things simple in order to minimize the stress level for everyone.

She'd also contacted Marge Kaufmann to make sure the wedding and groom's cakes would be done on time and then called the caterer about the final food preparations for the 25th.

***

Minnie's funeral ceremony was quite elaborate and took hours to complete. Hope and John were extremely proud of their son as he accepted the position of honorary shaman from the tribal elders. Alex was later called into their main office and presented with a scholarship to help with his career in medicine. The Tonkawa tribe had set aside some money from their gaming facility to help a few of their promising young people get an education.

Burton had given the ancient parchment to John so that it could be presented to the elders of the tribe. Alex had looked it over, but it made no sense to him. Minnie had died before she could see it, so their only recourse was to ask for help from the oldest members of their family. Alex still had El Mocho's mummified ear, but he and his father agreed to keep it for the time-being.

John and his family stayed with relatives at Fort Oakland the night of Minnie's funeral. Hope and the girls helped with the cooking and clean-up while John and Alex visited with Minnie's elderly cousin, Grey Fox. Grey Fox and Alex hit it off immediately and talked late into the night.

The next morning as Alex's family made preparations to leave, Grey Fox put his arm around Alex and said, "You will return soon to receive your Tonkawa name. Our tribal council meets in a few more days. We will discuss this matter then and let you know when to come back. Your grandmother would be very proud of you, my son."

John looked up at the darkening sky and hastened everyone into the car. Before long, they were on Interstate 35 heading south back to Texas. A strong, north wind pushed them as far as the Red River before letting up. Thankful that tornado season had ended, John drove on.

***

Nancy and Little Dove sat for a long while over their breakfast before getting dressed and driving the few miles to Nancy's old house. They were in Little Dove's SUV because it was bigger than Nancy's Honda.

Nancy tried hard to suppress her feelings, but tears streamed down her face anyway. She didn't know what made her the saddest, the wasted years with Black Tooth, his wasted life—or his death. What she did know was that she would never let anyone again treat her the way he had. She would now make her own decisions and be her own person.

Silently, the two sisters went through the house collecting the few items precious to Nancy. She took only things given to her by her family, wanting nothing to remind her of Black Tooth and the poverty he'd kept her in.

Finally, Little Dove could stand the silence no longer and asked, "Nancy, do you have any thoughts about where you will live now?"

"Yes, but I will tell you later when I am sure. Let's load the car and head on over to Big Elk's place. After today, I will not return to either house. They will be sold 'as is' with whatever is left behind. The darkness within their walls burdens my very soul."

Chapter Fifteen

EARLY TUESDAY MORNING, BURTON RECEIVED a call from his oldest son, Sean, in Ohio. "Hey, Dad. How are things going? Ready to tie the knot?"

"Sean! Good to hear from you. Everything's on schedule as far as I know, and it's now or never."

"Great. Listen, Dad, Amy and I have a problem. Her mother fell and broke her ankle yesterday. She had to have surgery, but she's doing fine. The only problem is that Amy's sister has to leave on Thursday and we have to get back here to take over. I guess what I'm saying is that we can be there for Thanksgiving, but we'll miss the wedding."

"Well, son, you'll do what you have to do. Joan and I will definitely miss you, but life goes on."

"There's something else, Dad. Michael is here and plans to drive down with Amy and me. That means he'll have to leave when we do too. I'm really sorry."

***

"No, Burton, we will not get married without your sons being

137

here. We'll just move the wedding up a day, that's all. I'll call the caterer, the preacher and a few others and it'll be just fine. You'll see."

I didn't give him time for a rebuttal, just turned and walked next door to give my daughter the news.

"Mornin', Mom," came a sleepy response when I walked into Sandra's kitchen. "What're you doin' over here so early? Is everything okay?"

"Mornin' Sugar. Just wondering how flexible your schedule is this week? Think we can do Thanksgiving and a wedding on the same day?"

"What did you just say?" she groggily mumbled.

After my brief explanation, she agreed it could be done. "I doubt the caterer will want to work on Thanksgiving Day, but if they'll just cook the food, Jack and I can pick it up around noon. Better call Marge about the cakes," and on and on she went.

I just stood there and smiled.

"What's that goofy look all about?"

"I'm just thinking how lucky I am to have a wonderful daughter like you living next door, that's all!"

"Well, don't just stand there gawking at me, let's make a list and delegate. Bobby and Karen will be glad to help out, too. Come to think of it, the schedule change will actually make things easier if we can pull it off. Good thing I'm off work tomorrow."

***

The Chief walked Nancy out of his office and past Nioka's tidy desk. They stopped a moment as he gave his long-time secretary instructions. "Nioka, Nancy has decided to sell Black Tooth's and Big Elk's houses and property. I told her we would act on her behalf and let her know when there is a buyer for either or both properties. I've already given her money for Black Tooth's pickup, and we'll simply take up the payments. The department needed a new truck anyway, so this made it easy for both of us."

"Do you know where you'll be living now, Nancy?" inquired Nioka.

"Only temporarily. I'll leave my cell phone number and the number for the house I'll be staying in down in Texas. My new friend, Joan, is getting married and I'm going to house-sit for her while she's on her honeymoon. After that, who knows?"

"Honey, whatever you decide we'll accept, but know you'll always have a place here on the reservation."

Nancy doubted that, but she hugged both of them warmly and walked out to her loaded-down car. Without so much as a peek in the rear-view mirror, she drove away, leaving behind as much of her past as she could.

***

I heard a loud knock on my front door and glanced up at the kitchen clock—10:00 it read.I wasn't expecting any company, so wondered who it could be. Drying my wet hands on a cup towel, I shuffled through the living room and peeked out the window. My son was standing on the front porch with a large package in his arms.

"Bobby! What on earth are you doing out here this morning? I didn't think I'd see you 'til tomorrow."

"Well, hello to you, too!" he laughed. "Can't a man see his mother the day before her wedding, or is that against the rules?"

"Of course he can, come on in. I imagine I'll be seeing Burton shortly as well--we don't hold with too many wedding superstitions around here."

We exchanged hugs and looked each other over lovingly. I brushed a shock of overly-long hair from his brown eyes and kissed his bearded face. "Don't worry, Karen's gonna cut my hair before tomorrow. Can't have a shaggy son walking you down the aisle!"

"I didn't say anything………."

"You didn't have to, I know that look! Anyway, Karen wanted me to bring our gift on over today so we'll have one less thing to worry about tomorrow with the kids and all."

"Is that the only reason you came? That's a pretty long drive just to deliver a gift."

"Actually… I'm not supposed to answer that question, Mom," he sheepishly replied.

"I see………… so why don't you come into the kitchen and have some coffee and cinnamon rolls? Nancy put some in the freezer before she left, so I thawed them out this morning. I'll put the gift with the others in the living room."

"Who's Nancy?" he asked as he picked up a delicious morsel and stuck it into his mouth.

"Oh, thought I told you. She's Burton's friend's relative. Long story, but she needed a place to stay during a family emergency. I said she could stay with me. She's also the one who'll be house-sitting while we're on our honeymoon. She should be back some time this evening-- had to take care of some business in Oklahoma. Anyway, Nancy is an awesome cook."

"I'll have to agree with you on that," he confirmed as he pulled another yeasty roll away from its sticky companions and licked his fingers loudly."

"What are you two agreeing on?"

Bobby and I both looked up as Burton quickly entered from the back door, wiped his boots on the doormat, and removed his hunting jacket.

With a sly look, my son answered, "....that these are the best cinnamon rolls I've ever put in my mouth."

My future husband slapped Bobby on the back, reached over his shoulder and helped himself, "Gotta agree with you there, son."

As I got my hug, Burton sheepishly said, "Mmmm....thought you had a hair appointment today."

Glancing between my fiancé and my son, I could see they had a conspiracy going. "I do have an appointment this afternoon. Why do you ask?"

"No particular reason, just wondering," he replied with mock innocence.

"Whatever it is you two are up to, I'll be out of your hair right after I fix lunch."

A few minutes later, Burton and Bobby excused themselves to the barn. Jack's pickup was backed up to the large, double doors blocking my view. I was curious as to what my men-folk were doing, but didn't have time to worry much about it as I still had to get dressed, put on make-up, and get to the beauty shop on time.

Finally, I threw together some tuna fish sandwiches, quickly downed one of them, and yelled out the back door, " Guys, there's sandwiches on the kitchen counter. I've got to head into town!"

Burton stuck his head out of the barn to make sure I didn't head that way and answered back, "Thanks, Hon. Be careful. See you later."

***

It was 3:30 on Thanksgiving afternoon. Our wedding guests and family had all arrived and were gathered around the back yard in conversation. Fortunately, the weather cooperated so that we didn't have to move everything to the church. The thermometer on the patio read 70 degrees—perfect. Sunshine brought added warmth to the happy occasion, and thankfully, the breezy wind subsided.

As promised, I'd stayed out of the barn, so was clueless as to what had taken place there the day before. Sandra was in on the surprise and had sworn the girls to secrecy as well. They giggled in anticipation any time the word "barn" was mentioned.

Nancy had come in rather late the night before, but was up early to help out with a little cooking and decorating. She looked beautiful in the new clothes she'd bought for herself, and I couldn't help but think had sad I'd be when she had to leave.

She helped me get dressed and then straightened the back of my hair. "Joan, you look wonderful," she insisted as I fussed over some stray locks of hair and applied my lipstick.

While my back was turned, she pulled something out of her pocket and said, "Joan, do you have something 'borrowed'?"

"What do you mean?"

"You know, like the old saying goes —something borrowed to wear for your wedding."

"Well, no, I guess I hadn't thought much about it, why?"

She held up a beautiful Indian necklace and said, "This was my grandmother's necklace. I'd be honored if you would wear it during your wedding ceremony."

"Nancy, it matches my outfit perfectly. It's gorgeous!"

"I know. I brought it from my house in Fort Oakland. When I packed it, I thought it would work well with the colors in your outfit. So, you'll wear it?"

"Yes, yes, of course I'll wear it. It's beautiful. Thank you."

She put the necklace around my neck, and I watched her face light up with joy. It wasn't going to be easy to watch her walk away some day. She was a very special person, and I was growing very fond of her.

Taking a final look in the mirror, I said, "It's time, Nancy. Let's go."

Together, we walked into the kitchen and gazed out the long row of windows. Bobby was standing just outside the door to escort me down the long, rock path to the gazebo where Burton stood waiting. From this vantage point, I couldn't see Burton's face, but I could see that he was handsomely decked out in a western-cut suit with his spit-shined boots gleaming in the sunlight.

To his right, stood Sandra and Karen in their ankle-length mauve dresses. Each carried a single, long-stemmed golden rose. They were as beautiful as they were different. Sandra's blonde tresses made a great contrast to Karen's raven hair. Like trained models, I saw them plant a kiss on each of Burton's rugged cheeks and return to their places. Oh, my, I'm sure his head just got a little bigger......

Sean and Michael flanked Burton's left side as everyone faced the patio in anticipation. It was obvious who sired those two handsome young men. Michael wore his dress uniform, while Sean had on a simple, brown jacket and jeans.

Pastor Fettke held the Bible tightly in his left hand and stood to the right of the gazebo entrance. The asters and chrysanthemums surrounding the little building regally lifted their heads in celebration.

There was no music other than what was offered by Mother

Nature herself—and she performed well. The Yegua sent a fanfare my direction as Canadian Geese honked their way south. The cattle lowed in the back pasture, while in the yard, a few hungry cardinals chirped around the bird feeder.

Proudly, I took my son's strong arm and glanced around at all my friends and family gathered in the back yard. "Ready, Mom?" he grinned and then added, "You look gorgeous."

"Thanks, Son. Let's go before Burton changes his mind!"

Slowly, we followed the scented petals thrown in our path by Kassie and Emma who wore ankle-length dresses similar to the ones worn by Sandra and Karen. Justin, who took his part very seriously, walked between his cousins as the official ring bearer. His solemnity was in contrast to the girls who had engaged in an impromptu competition to see which of them could empty her flower basket first. Faster and faster they jumped over the rocky path as if they were in a game of hopscotch.

Bobby and I suppressed a laugh as we overheard Justin say, "Slow down, you gotta be regal like princesses!" Where he learned that term was beyond me, but it was certainly wasted on the girls. They reached the gazebo a good six feet ahead of him and took their places in front of Sandra. Looking out at the crowd, they smiled sweetly to let everyone know they'd completed their mission—and in record time!

As soon as we all thought the drama was over, Kassie noticed her basket was not empty after all. She plopped herself down on the gazebo floor and bounced her basket upside down until every petal dropped out.

"See, I beat you," Emma leaned over and whispered to her younger sibling.

In retaliation, Kassie grabbed Emma's basket and tossed it out of the gazebo. Before anyone could stop them, the girls were shoving each other and about to get into a real free-for-all. Sandra handed her rose over to Karen and bent over to separate the girls while Jack put down the video camera and ran to the gazebo to assist her.

Emma was finally repositioned beside Justin, Sandra kept a hand on Kassie's shoulder, and Bobby and I resumed our walk. What would happen next? A few more steps and I could see Burton's face clearly. His beautiful smile was contagious and his enthusiasm over-powering. Impetuously, he left his assigned position, walked down the gazebo steps and headed towards me. When he met us, he gently took my arm from Bobby and placed it on his own.

"I'll finish this," was all he said.

We slowly walked the last twenty or so yards as everyone applauded. It was our moment, our time, and we enjoyed every minute of it.

As we stepped onto our "marriage rock" which now read November 24, 2012, I understood. "Thank you, Minnie," I whispered. "I don't know how you did it, or how you knew, but thank you for this gift."

Our feet left the rock and we approached the pastor, who was already speaking to us. What he said, I don't remember, but I do recall how I felt at that moment—happy, blessed, and complete.

After our vows were said and rings exchanged, Justin gave the final prayer and then added, "Nana, kiss your husband!"

Burton planted a very smoochy kiss right on my lips, to everyone's amusement. He then made his own announcement, "Joan and I want to thank all of you for making the sacrifice to be here on Thanksgiving Day to share our wedding vows. We understand that some of you had to forego your own plans to be here and we appreciate it very much. I'm especially proud to have both of my sons with us, along with Sean's fiancé, Amy. Now, if we can get the preacher to bless the food, we'll all head on out to the barn and eat!"

Nancy, Marge and Alfons had already made their way out to get the serving line started while the wedding party took a few more pictures.

Among our many wedding guests that day were John, Hope and their children. We were surprised they made it since they'd not been home from Minnie's funeral but a short time. They walked with the others to the barn for the reception. Soon everyone was inside sharing huge plates of barbeque and trimmings. Laughter echoed up and down the creek bottom as family and friends celebrated together. However, there was one wedding guest who wasn't celebrating. Before long, he slipped out, unnoticed, into the dusky evening.

***

He was sure no one saw him leave. They were too busy eating, talking, laughing--watching the Mosleys open up their wedding gifts. He'd simply pretended to refill his tea glass, walked on past the beverage table, and right out the door.

The graying sky would make it hard for anyone to see or follow him. Alex darted behind a row of cars lining the road in front of Joan's cabin. He needed twenty minutes—that was all—just twenty minutes. He'd be done and back inside the barn before he was missed.

Fingering his keys, Alex opened the truck of his car, pulled out a hand trowel, a small box, and quietly slammed the lid. Rather than go back through Joan's yard, he crawled over the barbed-wire fence beside Sandra and Jack's trailer. Inside, Cooter heard the commotion and began barking. "Hush!" Alex thought to himself. "Don't give me away now."

Once out of sight, the young Indian picked up his speed. It made him sad to think of the last time he'd run through this field. He was also a bit fearful. His hand grasped the leather pouch now around his neck. It held El Mocho's dried-up ear. Alex hoped he wouldn't hear the voices this time. They had been confusing before-- all talking at once in languages he didn't understand. If his grandmother had heard them, they didn't seem to bother her. But then, she was more at home in that "other" world than he would ever be.

Just another hundred yards, "Hurry, hurry!" he prompted himself. He'd brought along a flashlight just in case it got too dark to see what he was looking for. As he got closer, a cold sweat broke out across his dark face. He brushed the perspiration off with the back of his hand and continued. Suddenly, the ground became unstable beneath his feet, causing him to fall into a new plum thicket. He lay still for a second until the prickly shrubs brought him back to his senses. What had just happened?

Quickly, he got to his feet and glanced back at the barn to make sure no one had followed him. Good—he was still alone, or so he thought.

***

The photographer had finished our pictures in and around the gazebo and Burton and I lingered behind to share a few "sweet nothings" until we were summoned inside the barn. Finally, we were given the signal and headed that way. Burton escorted me across the yard and through the open double doors

As we entered, the emcee announced, "Ladies and gentlemen, I present to you, Mr. and Mrs. Burton Mosley!"

Everyone stood and applauded as we entered what used to be my old barn. Burton, Jack, and Bobby had somehow made that dilapidated, old building into a wonderland. The interior walls were completely covered in black plastic and curtains had been hung over that to give the illusion of a huge castle. From the ceiling hung three large chandeliers that gave a soft glow to the area.Flowers and candles decorated the tables, and the dirt floor was covered in cedar shavings.

"Oh, my goodness," was all that came out from my mouth. "Oh, my goodness!"

"Well, what do you think?" asked my confused husband.

"It's unbelievable. How on earth you managed all this in such a short time is beyond me. I love it!"

"Good. For a minute, I thought you were disappointed."

"Never!"

Before anything else was said, the music started, and we were instructed to have our first dance as man and wife out on the wooden platform that had been erected especially for the occasion.

That done, the music continued as we took our places at the head table and were served our plates.

Marge had done an awesome job on both cakes. The wedding cake was three-tiered and covered in sugary yellow roses. Burton's cake was Irish Rum and decorated in a hunting theme.

The music continued as we finished our barbeque and headed over to the cake table for pictures. Several couples braved the dance floor, including Burton's two sons. Sean danced with his fiancé, Amy, while Michael waltzed with Emma and Kassie at the same time—much to their delight.

Soon our cakes were cut and served to our guests who seemed to be enjoying themselves. Marge and Alfons had brought along his single cousin, George, who was visiting from Austin. Apparently George had already met Nancy since I saw him approach her table and invite her to dance.

Seeing her hesitation, I inwardly thought, "Go for it, girl, go!"

It must've worked because she awkwardly gave him her hand and walked to the dance floor with him. Burton saw me staring and tugged on my arm. "Stay out of this, Joan."

"What on earth are you talking about?" I innocently replied.

"You know very well what I'm talking about — no matchmaking."

"Looks like there's not much left for me to do," I quipped right back with a smile.

***

Alex quickly dug a hole over El Mocho's old grave to reunite the ear with the dusty remains of his body. As Alex placed the disfigured ear into the hole, an unseen force grabbed hold of his arm and held on. Alex struggled to free himself, but was unable to do so. "Who are you and what do you want?" he asked with a quivering voice.

The eerie answer came deep from under Alex's feet. The language he didn't recognize, but the meaning was clear. "Do not disturb me again—leave me in peace and be gone from here!"

With that said, Alex's arm was released and he fell backwards. As soon as he could breathe again, he picked up his things and ran away as fast as his strong legs would take him.

Chapter Sixteen

AFTER ALL OF OUR GUESTS left, Burton and I were left alone in the cabin. Nancy had moved out to Burton's travel trailer to give us some privacy until we left the next day for our honeymoon cruise.

Although we'd been alone together many times, this was different. We were now man and wife, and with that came certain privileges— privileges we had not taken advantage of until now. I'm not sure which one of us was more nervous—me or Burton.

***

Nancy stared up at the ceiling in Burton's trailer for what seemed to be hours. It wasn't that she couldn't get comfortable; she just couldn't stop her mind from replaying the evening's events. She didn't know what to make of Alfon's cousin, George. He seemed to really like her and she had certainly enjoyed the few dances they'd shared.

George had asked for her phone number—and she'd given it to him. What would her mother had thought if she were still alive? Her daughter dating a white man......oh, that would not go over well at all. No matter that the Indian she'd been married to treated her like a slave—that was different.

She'd have to call Little Dove in the morning and get her advice. Little Dove always steered her in the right direction. Hadn't she advised her NOT to marry Black Tooth? It wasn't as if she had really loved Black Tooth either. Nancy's mother and Black Tooth's mother had more or less prearranged things, giving Nancy little choice in the matter, short of running away from home. Being the obedient daughter she'd been raised up to be, she went through with her mother's plans-- and lived to regret it.

***

Alex drove slowly back to the A&M campus in College Station. He replayed the strange events from the past month over and over again in his head. What was of this world and what wasn't? He wasn't sure any more, and without Minnie to guide him, he felt isolated—in limbo between two worlds, neither of which he fit into. His father didn't seem to understand him, and his mother was so busy with his sisters that he didn't want to bother her with his problems.

Even worse, he had no one at school to confide in. He was already considered "different" by some, even though he excelled on the soccer team and worked part-time for one of his professors. Maybe he should talk to one of the older chiefs from his tribe in Oklahoma. Certainly one of them could help him understand the strange events he'd witnessed recently—help him put his world into perspective.

Putting those thoughts behind him for the time-being, Alex retrieved his bag from the trunk and jogged up the steps to the dorm. Classes started again in the morning, and he needed to finish a paper that had been assigned before the Thanksgiving holidays had begun.

In two and a half more weeks, the semester would be finished, and he could make the trip to Fort Oakland and hopefully, get some answers. Since he hadn't given his parents a definite time to be home for the Christmas holidays, they wouldn't miss him for a few days.

***

Being newlyweds, Burton and I took our time getting up Friday morning. We were both a bit overwhelmed from the night before and giggled like a couple of teenagers in love for the first time. Even though I'd been married before, I discovered that I was extremely bashful in front of my new husband. He, on the other hand, seemed to have no self-inflicted inhibitions.

We lingered a bit longer, basking in our new-found intimacy, as his stubbly beard rubbed against my sensitive skin. Reluctant to move, I said, "You know, we do need to get up and get moving so we'll make our flight on time."

"Mm-hym," was Burton's lazy reply as he nibbled my earlobe again.

"Okay, buster, I mean business this time!" Quickly, I escaped his grasp and ran for the shower.

"Wait for me!" he laughed.

Thirty minutes later, we made it to the kitchen only to discover that Nancy had slipped in sometime earlier and brought us a honeymoon breakfast. A little later, Sandra brought over some soup and sandwiches for our lunch. Both made it in and out without being detected.

"I could get used to this," I thought to myself, "the loving—and the food!"

Soon after lunch, the rush was on to get to the Austin airport. We allowed an extra hour to get through all the checkpoints due to the Thanksgiving crowd. Good thing since our flight boarded shortly after we got to our gate.

The plane touched down in Miami just as the sun was setting in the west. After gathering our luggage, we found a taxi to take us to our hotel and settled in before finding a good restaurant for our evening meal.

"What are you hungry for?" my new husband tenderly asked.

"I'm thinking seafood. How 'bout you?"

"Sounds good to me. It oughta be fresh considering where we are."

We took the elevator down to the lobby and located the concierge who advised us where to eat. Luckily for us, a terrific seafood restaurant was just around the corner allowing us to stretch our legs a bit.

Burton and I were seated in a quiet little nook by the back windows of the restaurant. From there, we could see Christmas lights lining the street while shoppers took advantage of the good weather to buy those first gifts. Christmas—it was too early to even think about that, but then again, we might find some nifty presents at some of the ports along our cruise route.

While we waited for our food to be served, Burton and I looked over the itinerary we'd received in the mail a few weeks earlier. We decided we could handle snorkeling in the Bahamas, but passed on parasailing and scuba diving. We also agreed that most of our water activities would take place on the cruise ship since their pools were heated! Being Texans, we were used to swimming when the outdoor temperature was 100 degrees, not a cool 75-80 degrees.

After an awesome lobster dinner, we took a stroll up the street to window shop and let our food settle. We didn't stay long since we wanted to get to bed early. Our ship sailed out of the harbor early the next morning and we didn't want to miss it.

***

She put on her favorite jeans and the new sweater she'd found at that cute little shop at the mall in Round Rock. Next, she twisted her long, black hair into a knot and pinned it into place. Earrings and a matching necklace sat on the dresser waiting for her to put them on after a splash of her new perfume.

Nancy sat down to pull on her knee-high boots and then stood to take a final look in the full-length mirror. Yep, she'd shed a few pounds the past couple of weeks alright. That was good. George didn't seem to mind a few extra pounds, but she wanted to look her best.

It felt strange to be going out on a date. Protocol insisted she mourn the death of her husband, but who was there to make her? Black Tooth had been a terrible husband—a cruel husband. No, she would not mourn him. She would go out on this date AND she would have a good time.

As she took another look in the mirror, Nancy heard Cooter announcing George's arrival. She grabbed up her purse and headed to the front door of the cabin as George's truck came to a stop. She waited for his knock and then opened the door, "Hello, George. Are we ready to go, or would you like to come in for a minute?"

"Wow!" was all the shy George could muster.

Nancy basked in his attention and grabbed his arm. Together, they walked to the pickup and he opened the door for her. He couldn't help but admire her ample backside as he helped her up on the running board and into her seat.

***

As our plane circled the Austin airport, our honeymoon officially ended. But, it was also good to be home. Burton and I struggled with our overstuffed bags as we stepped up into the airport tram that would take us to the parking lot. Thankfully, we'd remembered to pack our jackets close to the top of our luggage and pulled them out at the last minute. At forty-two degrees, it was cold! Two weeks in the Caribbean and we were spoiled.

I called Sandra as soon as we sat down. "Hey, Hon. Just letting you know we've landed and are headed home. Everything okay there?"

"Hey, Mom! Yeah, we're all fine. We missed you, but know you had a great time. We'll want details when you get here!"

"Done! We're starving and will eat on the way home, so don't worry about cooking anything, okay?"

"Sounds good to me. Drive safely!"

***

When Burton and I came up the driveway, we could see smoke curling its way out of our chimney. There was a strange pickup parked out back and all the lights were on in the cabin. We exchanged surprised looks and parked in front instead of the side carport.

Before we could get out of the car, the front door burst open and my two granddaughters pushed their way through with Cooter on their heels. "What didja bring us, Nana?" yelled Kassie.

"You're not spose ta ask that, you ninny," reprimanded Emma.

"I see nothing's changed much since we left," I laughed, "but we did bring you a surprise. Give us a minute to get our luggage."

The girls escorted both Burton and me inside where we found Sandra, Jack, Nancy, and another semi-familiar face. "Welcome home!" they all yelled simultaneously.

"I baked a cake and there's some coffee in the kitchen," offered the ever-helpful Nancy. "You remember George, Alfon's cousin?"

"Of course. Glad to see you, George," we said and shook his hand. After a round of hugs, we finally all sat down together near the fireplace.

Soon our coffee mugs were filled, as well as our plates, and Burton and I shared our adventures with the group while the girls played with their new toys.

About an hour later, Sandra and Jack left to put Emma and Kassie to bed. Cooter followed close behind. Nancy informed us that she was sleeping in the trailer—said our honeymoon hadn't ended yet. George put his arm around Nancy and walked her outside. Burton and I exchanged a sly smile and went to bed.

***

Alex hadn't counted on the traffic being so heavy on I-35 going through the Dallas/Ft. Worth metroplex. Before, he'd always been a passenger in his parents' car, not actually doing the driving. In fact, this was the longest trip he'd ever taken by himself. It felt kinda good to be on his own, to take charge of his life.

Maybe he would stop at one of the big malls on the way back and pick up some presents for his parents and sisters. He had a little extra cash from his job at school. He had been frugal with his money—not blowing it like he'd seen so many of his classmates do.

The Tonkawa Tribe always held its tribal council meetings in early December and he'd gone a couple of times when his father drove Minnie up for them. This year, they'd gone up for her funeral, not a tribal meeting.

Sad thoughts filled Alex's active, young brain as he continued to drive his little sports car north toward the reservation. He decided that he would stop for lunch not long after crossing the Red River. Not having anyone to talk to save himself, he was a bit bored and getting very hungry. In his determination to push onward, he naively ignored the graying sky ahead.

An hour and a half later, Alex saw a busy truck stop and decided that was where he would eat. His father had always told him to look for the busy ones and he'd find good food.

After a restroom break, Alex scooted into an empty booth near a small TV set suspended from the ceiling. Glancing around the room, he saw a number of truckers casually talking, eating and playing video games on bar stools.

A twenty-something, curvaceous waitress smiled and brought him a grease-stained menu along with a glass of water. "Well, hello, darlin'. What's a good-lookin kid like you doing out all alone in this weather?"

Not being used to flirtation, Alex ducked his handsome head and mumbled something about going to visit relatives further north.

"Honey, you ain't planning ta drive north tonight are ya? Haven't ya been listnin' to the weather? Look round this room. See all these here truckers. Most of em ain't goin' nowhere til it clears up. There's a good, ole norther comin through and it's supposed ta be bringin some sleet and snow with it. Sweetie Pie, you better be finding yerself a place to spend the night. Say.......I know where you kin stay........."

Not knowing how to respond, Alex blushed and said he'd be moving on, norther or not, and that he was ready to order his food.

Nellie sweetly smiled down at the half-man, half-boy child and put a manicured finger under his chin. "Whatever you say, darlin'. Whatcha wanna eat?"

As Nellie's full hips swayed back to the kitchen, Alex's attention was drawn back to the weatherman on the little television set. He couldn't quite hear what he was saying due to the noise in the room, but it was obvious a storm was on the way.

***

Burton and I sat alone in our kitchen recapping all the fun we'd had on our honeymoon. It was a crisp, cool morning with a hint of bad weather to come. Having been away from a television for the past two weeks, we hadn't felt the need to turn ours on and sat savoring our second and third cups of coffee in blissful peace.

Finally, I said, "Burton, do you know what today is?"

Well, yes, as a matter of fact, I do," he smugly said. "It is Monday, December the twelfth."

"You know that's not what I mean, silly. One year ago, you and I put up our first Christmas tree together and I'm thinking that maybe we should do that again today. Whataya say?"

Looking out the window at the darkening sky, Burton shook his head and said, "I don't know, Sunshine. It looks like it could get nasty out there before long."

"We don't have to walk; let's just take the Ranger out and cut down a tree by the north bend of the Yegua before the rain sets in. There's several nice cedars over there that are just about the right size. It won't take very long, and we can have our tree up before dark."

"What about the bridge? We can't drive across it, and the little ravine is too muddy."

"Jack was supposed to fix the bridge while we were gone on our trip, so I don't think it'll be a problem."

With that settled, we changed topics and began to discuss our new friend, Nancy. "So, do you think she and George are serious?" I asked.

"Who knows, but from the way he looked at her last night, I'd say so."

"Burton, I don't want her to leave, and from what she tells me, she doesn't want to return to Oklahoma—too many bad memories there."

"I suppose she could stay in the trailer, but it's going to get mighty cold out there soon. The cabin's too small to be comfortable for all of us, but she could sleep here when the weather's bad—like I think it'll be tonight."

"Good! I'll tell her right after we cut down our tree. Maybe she'd like to help us decorate it."

***

Ignoring the weatherman and the waitress, Alex paid his bill and walked out into a blustery north wind to his car. Alex was a very intelligent young man, but, like so many other youth, felt he was invincible and decided to plunge forward into the storm. He pulled his jacket closer and zipped it shut. Checking his fuel-gauge, he decided he'd better fill up before getting back on the interstate.

At the last minute, Alex ran back inside the truck stop and bought some snacks and bottles of water—just in case.

In many ways, Alex was a lot like his grandmother. Minnie had always been a force to be reckoned with, and he had apparently inherited her temerity. He was on a quest to seek his destiny in the world of medicine—whether it be the white man's, the Indian's, or both. No little snow storm would stop him from making this trip north to the reservation to talk to Grey Fox and the elders of the tribe.

***

Later that afternoon, Nancy sat in the kitchen sharing a cup of hot tea and some cookies with me. Burton had gone out to the barn to find the Christmas tree holder and trim the tree to fit.

"Nancy, Burton and I want you to stay with us as long as you want. You can use the travel trailer for your personal space and sleep in our extra bedroom when it's cold or if you feel lonely. And, by-the-way, it will be very cold tonight, so plan to sleep over."

"Yes, yes, I do want to stay, Joan, but you must let me earn my keep by cooking and cleaning."

"Okay, if that will make you feel better, but you don't have to, you know."

"No, it's the only way I'd stay. I wouldn't feel right otherwise. Besides......"

"Besides, what?" I prompted.

"Well, uh, I think I'm getting married."

"Married!" I shouted.

"Yes, George and I have been dating and doing a lot of talking while you and Burton were on your honeymoon, and we both feel this is where we're headed."

"But, you've only known each other three weeks!"

"I know. We won't marry right away. Alfons has made George an offer he feels he must take being as Alfons has no son to help him. Besides, George was given notification that his job will no longer exist after the first of the year. Like me, he has no where else to go."

"What exactly are you talking about? Neither Marge or Alfons has said anything about this."

"Alfons is giving George fifty acres of land. George is to build a house, live here and help run the farm with Marge and Alfons. He has also agreed to take care of them in their old age since they have no other heirs to help them. When they pass on, he'll inherit everything. He wants me to be his helpmate—his wife."

"Nancy! This is wonderful. Then you won't have to leave. Burton and I were both dreading the time when you'd return to Oklahoma."

"Never! I want to forget my life with Black Tooth. Unlike George, Black Tooth treated me as his property—never as an equal. No, I'll never go back there."

***

Mixed snow and sleet hit Alex's windshield at an angle, making it hard to keep his equilibrium on the slippery highway. Telephone poles lined the road, their wires coated in ice. Why hadn't he heeded the waitress's warning? Was it that he was too proud, too sure of himself? His little car was quickly becoming no match for the sudden bursts of wind that made the snow swirl around in front of him.

He was glad he'd filled his tank with gas and bought some food. The next town was a good twenty miles away and he was beginning to doubt he could get there. There had been only one vehicle to pass him in the past fifteen minutes and that was a four-wheel drive Jeep. The reservation was a good two hours north of his present position. What to do? He could always turn around and head back to the truck stop, but then he might be stuck there for days. No—he'd push on. His parents expected him home in a few days and he didn't want to disappoint them.

Alex soon realized the error of his thinking when he could no longer see the center stripe on the highway. He was out in the middle of nowhere and there certainly had not been any snowplows out clearing the roads. Darkness was falling, giving him a real sense of urgency. Up ahead, he could see the dim outline of the next town's lights and vowed he would stop there for the night—if he could make it.

Without warning, Alex's car hit a slick spot and went into a tailspin. He slid off the road and into a frozen bar-ditch. He tried desperately to drive himself out of the ditch, but there was no traction and he was stranded . "Okay, no problem," he said aloud to no one. "I'll just call 911 and they'll send out a wrecker for me."

His plan would've worked had there been a cell phone tower close by. Over and over, the call refused to go through. In frustration, he got out of the car and walked several different directions in search of a signal—all to no avail. Teeth chattering, Alex made a hasty retreat back to the car to escape the harsh wind and snow. He should've listened to that waitress back at the truck stop........

***

About seventy-five miles away, Grey Fox solemnly put down his coffee mug and announced to his wife, "Owl Eyes is in trouble."

"Who is Owl Eyes?" she asked.

"John's son, Alex. We have chosen the name Owl Eyes because he is wise for his age. He was to take our cousin's place as a healer, but she died before she could finish the task of teaching him."

"How do you know he is in trouble?" his wife continued.

"Minnie just told me."

"Minnie? How?"

"I'm not sure how she did it, but her words are in my mind. I will call together the elders and together we will decide how to help Owl Eyes."

"You cannot go out in this weather, Grey Fox! You are frail now, and it will make you sicker."

"I must help our little brother now. It is urgent. I will be fine."

***

"Hello, Grey Fox. How are you?"

A few seconds later, Hope overheard her husband reply, "No,

Alex has not come home from school yet. We assumed his exams were not done with. Why do you ask?"

By now, Hope was clinging to her husband's arm in anticipation of Grey Fox's reply.

"I'll try his cell phone and his dorm. I'll call you back in a minute."

"John, what's wrong? Why has Grey Fox called here looking for Alex?"

"It may be nothing, Hope, but Grey Fox has had a vision of Alex being trapped inside of something—said the vision came from Mother."

The call to Alex's cell phone went straight to his voice box and no one at Alex's dorm had seen him since the day before. John put his arms around his wife to comfort her and then called Grey Fox back.

"Grey Fox, Alex is not answering his cell phone and hasn't been seen in College Station since yesterday. We don't have any idea where he could have gone."

"I do, John. He is somewhere between College Station and Fort Oakland, but probably closer to us than you. In my vision, he was trapped inside a snowy place—and we've been in a blizzard for the past few hours. If he was on Interstate 35, he's probably stranded somewhere. Any idea why he'd be driving up here at this time?"

"Not exactly. I know he's had some hair-raising experiences with the spirit world lately and Mother's death was hard on him. After we visited with you, he told us he felt a certain bond with you—felt he could trust you. Alex doesn't trust very easily, so if he said those things, he meant them. Maybe he was coming to see you."

***

Back at the truck stop, Nellie happened to look up at the TV long enough to see a picture of Alex being flashed across the screen. Missing! She quickly put out her cigarette and pulled her cell phone out of her pocket. Her nimble fingers dialed the number scrolling across the picture and she waited for someone to pick up.

"The kid on TV—he was here 'bout an hour ago. Warned em not ta keep travlin' in this weather, but he took out anyways." That said, she continued on to give her location and a description of the car Alex drove. She put the phone back in her pocket and said a silent prayer for his safety. "Hardheaded kid," she said to herself, "done gone an got hisself in trouble."

***

Alex left the window cracked just enough to get some fresh air into the car. He cranked up the motor every few minutes to use the heater. His watch now read 7:30 p.m. It was really cold now so he decided to get his suitcase out of the back and put on all the clothes he could find to keep warm.

He unlocked the door and gave it a push but nothing happened. Darn the luck, the door was frozen solid. He could kick out the window, but then would be even worse off.

Giving in to hunger, he opened a package of peanuts and downed them with a bottle of water.

Not a single car or truck had passed since he'd run off the road. Most likely, he'd have to spend the night in the ditch. He just hoped someone would find him soon or he'd run out of gas and out of heat. After that........

To pass the time, Alex listened to the radio and at times, sang along with it. Finally, he came across the weather forecast for northern Oklahoma and listened in. It was even worse than he thought. More snow with temperatures dipping into the single digits for the night.

Chapter Seventeen

GREY FOX HAD BEEN HOME about fifteen minutes when the phone rang. It was the Oklahoma State Police telling him that a waitress in a truck stop on I-35 had seen Alex earlier in the day. Said the boy was determined to head north in spite of her warnings about the weather. He hadn't given her any information other than he was going to visit relatives.

Calculating the time Alex was at the truck stop and the effects of the weather on driving speed, Grey Fox figured he was somewhere south of Oklahoma City. The police were already searching for him, but Grey Fox knew that without help, they might not find him in time.

Against his wife's wishes, Grey Fox called several of the younger tribesmen and, together, they formed a rescue squad. Survival equipment was quickly thrown into the four-wheel drive pickup and they headed for the highway. Soon they were driving south on the interstate, but the going was extremely slow.

***

Burton carried the cedar tree into the cabin and set it up in the corner of the room. We had invited Nancy and George over for supper, and together, would decorate the tree.

Nancy insisted on cooking, so Burton and I brought down the Christmas decorations from the attic. It was hard to believe that a year earlier we hardly knew each other. It seemed we had been together for years—but it hadn't been so long, really. Last year at this time, I still ached for my beloved Heb, and had mixed emotions about my present husband. Ahhh......well, no time to get melancholy. It was Christmas and I was a very lucky woman to have a man like Burton by my side.

Soon, I began wrapping the gifts we'd brought back from the Caribbean while Burton went outside to find Jack and help feed the cows. Not to be left behind, Emma and Kassie climbed into the back seat of the pickup with Cooter, and off they all went. I watched as they drove across the pasture and sent up a quick prayer thanking God for bringing my daughter's family to live next door to me.

Before long, the last gift was wrapped and under the tree, and the aroma from the kitchen got my attention.

"Nancy, what are we having tonight? It smells scrumptious!"

"Bear-claw Soup," was her only reply.

"Seriously?"

"Of course."

"Please tell me there aren't any real bear claws in there."

Laughing, she replied, "Only because I couldn't find any!"

"Good! So, what's in there?"

Approving of Nancy's substituted ingredients, I offered to help, but was shooed out of the kitchen. Even though the sky was cloudy, I put on my hiking boots, grabbed my jacket, and went for a walk.

***

Later that evening, George arrived and we all sat down to a bowl of Bear-claw Soup and Nancy's home-made cornbread. She'd also thrown together a salad and made fried pies for dessert. She'd out-done herself, that was for sure.

"Mmmmm......this is the best meal I've had in ages," George commented between succulent bites.

"I'll have to agree with you, there, George," Burton added as he patted his expanding belly.

Looking up between spoonfuls of delicious soup, I saw Nancy sit up a little prouder, her olive complexion a little rosier. It was good to see her happy and no longer afraid of her own shadow. The thought of her no-good husband treating her so badly made me angry all over again. I was glad he was gone forever and couldn't hurt her any more. George, on the other hand, adored her. That was as clear as the nose on his ruddy face.

Finally, we finished our dessert, and Nancy poured us all a glass of wine. We toasted to good health, good cheer, joy to all, and waddled into the living room with the intentions of trimming the tree as soon as our dinner settled.

No sooner than we'd sat down, George stood up and raised his glass again. I'd like to make another proposal—this one is for Nancy. With that, the shy little man got down on one knee in front of his beloved and said, "Nancy, I know this is a bit sudden, but I'd be the happiest man in the world if you'd agree to be my wife. I'm not a rich man, but all I have is yours-- so whatta ya say?"

Tears filled Nancy's beautiful brown eyes as she dropped down on her knees beside George. She embraced him in a death-gripping hug and simply said, "Yes, George, yes."

Burton and I embraced the both of them and offered yet another toast. "To Nancy and George!" we sang out as our eyes met.

We both knew there must be something magical about the spot where they knelt as it was exactly where Burton knelt a year ago when he asked for my hand in marriage..........

***

The car engine sputtered to a halt, leaving Alex without any more heat. The battery still hadn't died, so he listened to a local radio station playing, "Silent Night." All he could do now was wait out the storm and hope someone would come by and see him. He didn't know how that would happen because the snow completely covered his car. Earlier, he'd looked through the glove box in search of anything that would be of use to him in this critical situation. A small flashlight was about the only thing that would help him tonight.

It wasn't much, and the batteries were weak, but he put it into his pocket and settled in for the night. If he heard a car come by, he'd turn on the light and kick out the window. He leaned the driver's seat back, relaxed a bit, and hoped for a miracle.

He meant to turn off the radio to save the car's battery, but fell into a drowsy slumber. An hour or so later, he awoke to find that his hands and feet were numb and the car battery completely dead. He jiggled his extremities as much as he could in the cramped space, but it didn't help much. He mentally beat himself up again for being so stupid.

Alex realized he was hungry and pulled out a candy bar from the grocery sack. He then took the top off of a bottle of water—both were frozen. Not a good sign.

Alex pushed the little button on his watch to illuminate the dial. It read 2:15. He didn't know how much more cold he could take. He nibbled slowly on the frozen chocolate and eventually went back to sleep. Wherever his vision took him was warm, and he could feel himself running, running—on four legs.

***

Grey Fox checked in with the State Police only to be told that there had been no signs of Alex's car. They would send out a helicopter at dawn if the wind had died down by that time. They had also checked for any signals coming from his cell phone and had found none.

Against police advice, Grey Fox and his crew continued south, creeping along, checking each snowdrift for signs of the young Tonkawa. They would've gone after him even if he wasn't the chosen medicine man for their tribe. He was family and they took care of their own.

"Grey Fox, are you sure we haven't missed him along the way?" asked Long Knife who was driving the truck. "I think we have plenty of fuel, but we don't want to pass him up and waste precious time."

"No, we have not missed him. We will find him."

"How can you be so sure? The snowdrifts are piled high everywhere. He could be inside any one of them."

No sooner than the young man asked this question, Grey Fox said, "See there. Follow the tracks."

None of the men in the pickup cab could believe what they were seeing. There, in the snow, were wolf tracks in the center of the south-bound lane.

They followed the tracks for another twenty minutes which then veered off to the left and circled a pile of snow down in the bar-ditch. Quickly, the men jumped out of the truck and began digging with their shovels. Soon, a little red sports car with a Texas license plate came into view. They dug faster, all the while calling Alex's name.

Finally, the windshield and driver's window were uncovered enough to see a body slumped over in the front seat. The men were more desperate now, fearing the worst. They pulled on the ice-covered door handle, but it refused to give way. With no other option clear to them, they carefully busted out the side window.

"He's alive! Quick, help me get him out!"

Alex's limp body was pulled through the window and onto the snow below it. His breathing was shallow, and the skin on his face had a deathly pallor.

The men quickly wrapped Alex in blankets and put him into the back seat of the dually with Grey Fox who held him tight. "Don't leave us now, Owl Eyes, we need you."

With as much haste as they dared, they proceeded to the nearest hospital in Oklahoma City. They then alerted the police as well as Alex's family.

***

It was two days before Hope and John could safely make the trip to Oklahoma to see Alex. They left his sisters behind with Hope's family so they would have room in the car to bring Alex home when he was healthy enough for the trip.

He was asleep when they entered his room. Hope could contain herself no longer and embraced him as best as she could without getting tangled up in his IV tube and catheter.

Alex's eyes opened slowly as he mumbled, "Mom, Dad……… ..I'm, I'm so sorry. I should've known better….."

"Son, we're glad you're alive, and, yes, I am terribly angry with you. I cannot imagine what possessed you to come up here in that blizzard—and especially without telling us. You almost died out there!" blurted John.

"If it hadn't been for Grey Fox and the others, I would be dead. I'm sorry I didn't tell you where I was going, but I really needed to see Grey Fox and ask him some questions—about my calling. I'm confused, and without Maw-maw, I don't know what to do."

"I guess I can understand that, Son, but next time, use your head. Talk to your mother and me. We may not have all the answers, but we are here for you."

Hope couldn't help but notice the bandages on her son's hands—frostbite. If his hands didn't heal, he may never become a doctor. She wondered if he knew this. He'd be lucky not to loose any toes or fingers according to the doctor. Time would tell.

While Hope pondered these things in her mind, she was vaguely aware of the conversation between her husband and son. They were now discussing his car and the damage it encountered from the slide into the ditch and the rescue team's efforts to free Alex.

"Dad, Grey Fox left before I could thank him. Can we call him now?"

"Certainly. He's in my address book--just a second.

Within seconds, Grey Fox answered his phone and spoke with John who then gave the phone over to Alex.

"Grey Fox, this is Alex. I want to thank you and the others who saved my life the other night. I don't know how to repay you, but I promise I'll do my best in school to become a doctor—a good doctor."

"Owl Eyes, that's what we're counting on!"

"Owl Eyes?"

"Yes, your Indian name—chosen by our elders."

"Why Owl Eyes?"

"Because we know that some day you will be wise like the owl, and you will use your eyes to see how to help your people."

"I don't feel very wise now, that's for sure, but I will learn as much as I can in school."

"Good!"

"One other thing, Grey Fox. How did you find me the other night?"

"I didn't.............your grandmother did."

***

Heb, it's me again. Everyone else is still asleep, but I wanted to come out here and wish you a Merry Christmas. This is the second holiday season we've had without you, and you're still missed very much. I guess you know that our grandchildren often climb up on your tombstone. Sometimes they're just playing, but maybe they're out here talking to you just like I do.

There have been many new beginnings this past year. Of course, my marriage to Burton has been the biggest event in my life recently, but Sandra and Jack are about ready to build their permanent home out here. I'm so glad they've decided to stay. They've been a real comfort to me and I've enjoyed having the girls nearby.

Bobby and Karen recently announced they're expecting another baby, and it's a girl this time. Justin was disappointed, but Kassie and Emma aren't. They've been picking out names just in case Bobby and Karen can't think of any good ones.

Seems our little Yegua family is growing and growing. Even Cooter has a girlfriend. She just showed up one day about a month ago. She looks like a miniature greyhound, so if she and Cooter have progeny, they'll be awfully strange-looking.

Our Indian friends got some good news recently too. Minnie's grandson, Alex, was missing and was found alive in Oklahoma. He was in the hospital for awhile, but came home yesterday to spend Christmas with his family. The Tonkawa tribe is sponsoring him as he studies medicine. They have drawn up plans for a health clinic and when Alex graduates from med-school, he will be their head physician.

You don't know Nancy, but she's a special friend who will soon become our neighbor on the south fence. She's marrying Alfon's cousin, George, and they'll be building their home at the same time as Sandra and Jack. As a matter of fact, Alfons, George, and Jack will do most of the work themselves. I imagine we'll all help out in one way or another.

Heb, it must have been destiny that brought us out here two years ago to help Minnie's family fulfill its purpose—come full-circle I guess. Nancy is from that same tribe. Her Tonkawa feet now walk the sacred grounds where her ancestors walked years ago. Like us, and many more to come, her spirit has been touched by the spirit of the Yegua.......